T0281951

Praise for *L*

"Did the narrator push her now comatose husband down those steps in Venice? Or is the truth far more slippery than that? Provocative, suspenseful, funny, poetic, and profound, *Life/Insurance* by Tara Deal explores the psyche of an unconventional woman and the complexities of love and marriage while invoking (among others): Nietzsche, García Márquez, Kerouac, Clarice Lispector, John Donne, Kate Bush, Soft Cell, and *Hagakure: The Book of the Samurai*. Original and rich in its use of a collage structure, its prose gemlike, Deal's novella is also an effortless and riveting must-read."

—Lyn Di Iorio, author of *Outside the Bones*

"Part interrogation, part dramatic monologue, *Life/Insurance* grapples with our biggest fears: meaning-making and uncertainty. How do you prove your worth when the values of others run counter to yours? What is a life worth to those living it versus the family members, critics, and claims adjusters who see things differently? A collage-like meditation on creativity, *Life/Insurance* raises questions about authenticity, intimacy, and identity. Deal builds an intricate and suspenseful mystery via a narrator who believes one has to break form—and oneself—to achieve."

—Margaret Luongo, author of *History of Art: Stories*

"Tara Deal's *Life/Insurance* is a masterful puzzle, a one-way conversation that poses more questions than it answers as a wife tries to communicate with her husband. This engaging journey into the lives of continent-hopping artists is riveting and Kafkaesque."

—Megan Staffel, author of *The Exit Coach* and *The Causative Factor*

"Tara Deal's *Life/Insurance* is an arresting meditation on memory, marriage, and art as well as our attempts to weave the broken threads of a life into a tapestry of meaning."

—Melissa Reddish, author of *The Lives We've Yet to Live*

"In this lyrical mental collage reminiscent of Virginia Woolf, a conversation emerges out of the strangely comforting and random thoughts of one woman who keeps asking questions. A colorful and compelling meditation on art and memory."

—Holly Pobis, artist/photographer

"Found beauty in a visual and lyrical mediascape. Red herrings and clues—a brush stroke, a rhythm or a spate of words—effortlessly invoke haiku, a song or a translucent collage, each advancing a darker narrative. On tenterhooks, we hypothesize the truth at the core of an irrevocable event."

—Lisa Kirchner, singer/songwriter

"Intricate, lyrical, dissonant, impossible to pin down, *Life/Insurance* is to be experienced as much as it is to be read."

—Jim Naremore, author of *The Arts of Legerdemain as Taught by Ghosts* and *American Still Life*

LIFE/INSURANCE

Tara Deal

Regal House Publishing

Published by
Regal House Publishing, LLC
Raleigh, NC 27605
All rights reserved

ISBN -13 (paperback): 9781646034901
ISBN -13 (epub): 9781646034918
Library of Congress Control Number: 2023950837

Cover images and design by © C. B. Royal

Regal House Publishing, LLC
https://regalhousepublishing.com

The following is a work of fiction created by the author. All names, individuals, characters, places, items, brands, events, etc. were either the product of the author or were used fictitiously. Any name, place, event, person, brand, or item, current or past, is entirely coincidental.

Printed in the United States of America

For Dan

If a question can be put at all, then it can also be answered.

—Wittgenstein, *Tractatus Logico-Philosophicus*

1

Blink if you can hear me. Blink twice. So I'll know it's not a random twitch. I'm sorry. Did I miss it? I was looking out of the window. Down the street. Trying to think of what. Steam is coming up from a vent. How are you going to get out of this? There are people wrapped up out there, wrapped up in things, and carrying cups of coffee. I should have brought you something. People outside are hurrying. They have no idea what's happening in here.

Your mother is in the hall, talking to a doctor. Crying to the doctor. I try to comfort her, but I don't know what to say. I tell her this won't last forever. Which doesn't help. She doesn't understand. She doesn't understand how you ended up here. She says: Idiot. And I don't know if she's talking to me. I think she thinks it's all my fault. She says: Your father died like an idiot too. That time, she was talking to you.

Sometimes, your mother forgets a word in English, and I have to figure out what she means, then translate.

Sometimes, I pretend I can't decipher, which drives her crazy.

But I know you know what she's saying. I'm sorry.

I need to get out of this room, soon. You know I have other things. No, that's not true. Don't worry, I'm not going to abandon you here, not like this, not now. I wouldn't do that to you. Even if you want me to. Even if you would have wanted me to, I mean, back then, back when you still loved me. When you first loved me, that is. I mean, what else can I do?

Do you remember what we used to do? Do you remember what happened? I don't know if I can explain it to your satisfaction. How much can you see from that position? Can you see out of the window? There's a deli across the street that sells lottery tickets. Does that mean anything? Do you know where we are? Does that give you a clue? Do you know what I'm talking about? Do you?

Accident while traveling. We were just tourists. Things crumble. People fall down. Your mother said we should have stayed home, here, where we belonged, and then something like this wouldn't have happened.

We ran, if you want to know the truth. And someone

got hurt. I was with you, right behind you, and here I am, still. It's not your fault. It was an accident, obviously.

Is this your worst-case scenario or mine?

What I mean is that I can't imagine what it's like for you. To be stuck, trapped, wrapped up in all these bandages. Unable. Do they have a balm? Are you going crazy? Or is it peaceful? When you close your eyes, does it feel like you're back in your dark blue room at home, where you could always shut the door and do whatever you wanted? Where you didn't have to answer my questions. My interrogations. And what are you doing now? What are you going to do about it? Are you composing a song?

Would you rather be alone? But you don't even have any music. I don't have anything to give you. Nothing to leave behind.

I know, I've tried, but they won't allow electronics in this room. Something about your brain and interference. It's ridiculous, but they are very strict about this rule. Nothing extraneous. Just me and you.

I'll be back tomorrow. I'll see what I can do.

Look: people brought you white roses and bagels.

People who don't really know what condition you're in. Someone should have told them something. Not necessarily the truth.

When I walked by the deli, I saw that the roses were still sitting in boxes on the sidewalk, waiting to be unloaded. Their names were stamped on the cardboard: Hope, Tibet, Lovely, and Alberta.

You wanted to go to Tibet, do you remember that? Or is that too much? Too much to ask. There was music there you wanted to hear. Something mountainous, elemental. There were certain instruments. But I don't know how you were going to use them. What you planned to do. How were you going to mix the ancient and the contemporary? You always ignored my questions. Do you still want to go there? Do you still care?

I mean, we have to go somewhere, eventually. Should we go together?

You're lucky. That's what everyone says. Most people in your situation would be dead. Most people could not survive a headlong fall down such a steep flight of foreign steps. Do you know what I mean? Your situation is special, that's what I'm saying. That's what everyone tells me.

They say to keep talking to you. It can't hurt. I might

discover something that will work. Something that will click. Something like a password that will do the trick. How to decide/decode?

Blink twice if you want me to continue.
    I'll come back tomorrow.
    I'll tell your mother to come in from the hall.
    It doesn't matter whether you want to see her or not.

It doesn't matter if you don't want to talk. But can you tell me one thing? Because there's just one thing I'd like to know, if that's possible. Do you remember what you told me? Right before your fall. Think back. You were listening to an interview with a new songwriter. While I thought we should be out on the streets, in the air, absorbing atmosphere, eating risotto. I wanted to walk through the twilight, pink and gray. It looked like a bit of art. But you liked to stay inside in the evenings. You always did. You always liked a small room with no view. Something like a cell. You didn't like to be bothered. You didn't like to be cross-examined. But that's not what I'm talking about right now.

And then you took off your headphones and told me about a songwriter who had done something new. You were always finding new music, while I was stuck with the old. I could never break out of that rut. This new songwriter had done something, but I don't know what. You told me something, in the middle of that palazzo apartment we had rented in the drizzle, but maybe I wasn't paying attention. So, now what I want to know is: What were you talking about? What were you trying to tell me? You didn't elaborate. You just said it. A sentence or two was all it took. We had rented that apartment for the whole month although who knew if we'd keep it.

Wasn't there someone who sang about all the things I should've said? (Kate Bush)

I'm sorry I'm so unoriginal. I was the one who said we should go to Venice, even though we'd been before. How many times has it been? But we could go again. You said you didn't mind. We were just another couple on vacation. A couple of tourists. We wouldn't make a scene.

You always said you'd go anywhere with me. You could compose in any country, in any kind of room. You had your headphones, and you liked to use them.

While you were working in your dark Venetian room, blinds drawn, before dinner, before we went out and everything fell apart, before you fell down those steps, I thought about that songwriter and thought—

I mean, tell me again what you were thinking. Were you trying to make a choice? Was it too difficult to devote yourself to two things at once? Did you think you had to give something up? Or sacrifice yourself? No one would have wanted that, then. And I don't think that's what you meant. You always said we could have it all. Or at least we could have a lot. Why not?

The doctor says we don't know if the fall caused your problem or if there was something that precipitated your fall.

The doctor says we have to give it some time. You might be able to go home. Not now, maybe later. It's hard to say when/what/how, however. In any case, they can't keep you here forever.

Last night, I cooked something from the cookbook that we bought in that bookshop by the canal, not the Grand Canal, something smaller. That shop is probably gone by now. Do you remember it? The cookbook, the canal, anything? Last night, I made pork belly with radicchio and hazelnuts. Or something like that. It seemed right at the time. How long has it been? I opened an old red wine. Plus, I had music in the background, and I sang along. The kind of music that you would never listen to. Is it wrong to continue my life while you're confined?

I did not invite your mother, however. Because I can't help her.

Every night after dinner, I walk the dogs. Then read books, late into the dark, as always, as before. Walking and reading. Back and forth, across the page, across the street, across the earth. I need the text. For my work. My collages, that's what I'm calling them. I am still gathering materials. Sometimes sentences from books, sometimes signs on the street. Sometimes warnings that people call out. Sometimes lyrics from songs that you never liked. I'm sorry, I can't help it. Sometimes, those other words are perfect.

I was always the reader. You were the writer. Songwriter, rather. Composer, you called it.

I was talking and you weren't listening. Those steps were so slippery. And then. A twitch, a glitch, a shadow. You turned around and I reached out. It doesn't matter.

We usually held hands while walking. It was so easy to get caught in the cobblestones. Or slip in the gutter. We always held hands across the gaps and grates. Through the wisps and gasps. What happened?

It would be nice if we could go back to Venice when this is finished. Or somewhere like that. Where would you like to go next? Some city or an island?

Just because you can't communicate (or, rather, won't) doesn't mean you can't think. You've revealed that much already. For a while, we thought you might want to write a book about it. About being stuck inside like this. Like that, I mean. You could blink out the words and sentences. I could write it all down for you. It would be a lot of work, but people have done it before. We could do it together. That would be something, wouldn't it? Even if there's already a book. You could write it all over again. It would be different. Wouldn't it?

But I know: your life was music. And you don't want to talk about it.

Rachmaninoff had three years of writer's block in which he couldn't compose a song. I read it in a magazine. I know you don't care about the old composers, but maybe his example provides some comfort? Your time here isn't wasted, maybe, that's what I'm trying to say. Are you composing in your head? Are we going to hear it one day? Do you remember that Rachmaninoff is buried in Westchester, in the same cemetery as your father? It's sad to think of Rachmaninoff in Westchester. Although I know people love it up there.

You were a composer, of a sort. What kind of composer? How many kinds are there? You never wrote lyrics, I know that much. You thought the music was sufficient. Was it? You thought music didn't have to make sense. Music didn't have to do anything. That must be nice, to have something like that in your life. Music just existed. Then evaporated. Music like cotton candy. But not sweet like that, of course not, that's not what I meant.

People used to praise your talent and ask me about it, trying to figure out what you do, what you're doing. And I always had to say I don't know anything about music. Except what I hear on the radio. Does that count?

I always told people that you were a composer of some sort. I don't know what kind exactly. I don't know what to call it. I'm sorry. Because now. There you are.

What's going to happen to your songs? I don't know how to access your files. Was there a special project? Something with an Italian reference? Do you want to give me the password or not? Are you worried about what I might do with everything you have stockpiled? That's not what you should worry about.

Italy was supposed to be good for my work, my art. For my collages, if that's what you want to call them. You said you didn't mind traveling. You could work in any kind of environment.

Maybe Venice would be a source of inspiration. Maybe it would trigger a variation. Or a series, that would be good. For both of us. Together or separately? We were always working on something. We couldn't help it, we were always trying to make something, make something up, make up for something, maybe. Other places always provided material. Although staying put in one place did as well. If you paid attention. We could have waited it out in New York. I could have continued. But we went.

We told people we were just going on vacation. Escape from the city. The same thing we always said when we left, unexpectedly. We were like tourists.

Your mother said we gave her heart an attack when we went somewhere without a plan. Something could happen. And what about the money? All this was too expensive. She thought I was taking advantage of you. Flying to foreign cities, lying on beaches, cheering at the bullfights. Your mother said it was too much. But how did she know what it was? You had already made enough money for both of us. She didn't understand. Where did it come from?

There is never enough music in the world, apparently. People always want something.

And with that kind of money, we could go anywhere, I mean, that's what we did, when we had the chance. We had to take it. Now, of course, we've stopped. At least we're in New York. Where we have to wait. For how long? I would tell you if I knew. I would tell you everything if I could.

The doctors tell me to keep doing what I am doing. They say to remember our life together. Talk as much as possible. Increase the volume. It might help. I might say the right thing. Something might turn the lock. Turn back the clock. Restart. They say you might be getting better. Although they have no answers. But they do have a timetable.

Do you remember the bullfights? You always went, wherever I wanted, whatever I suggested. Who knows what will be worth the effort? You could retreat to your dark room later, and I wouldn't bother you. We had an arrangement.

We watched the bull on his island of sand. Blood

dripping but ignore that, forget about the flesh, just for one minute, because what about that flash of yellow sequins, like a light bulb going on and off, right in front. Bulls have killed the matador before, of course, for less provocation than that. It could happen again. We waited in the stands. Do you remember how it ended?

Does it help to remember? Would you like to see a souvenir? There were so many things. There still are. And we've been together for so long now. Things are piling up. I don't know where to start. I mean, when to stop.

Don't worry, I'm not going to leave you. I'm not going to leave you here, of course not, that's not what I'm talking about. That would look suspicious. Plus, your mother would kill me.

I'll be back tomorrow.

I put on my hood when I leave your room and hope I don't run into people who want to talk about how you're doing. What you're doing. Are you doing anything? I can't tell. I can't tell them. Neighbors and doormen. They feel sorry for me.

They see that I am alone with two dogs. They know that you used to walk with me, in the evenings, once in a while, not always. They know that we used to work at home together, sharing the same space and time, which was unusual. Someone said it was admirable. How did we do it? We must have figured out a routine. We must have had separate rooms. Everyone always wanted to know: what did we do? You were a composer, but I could never elaborate. Sometimes, someone who knew a lot about music wanted to ask some questions. Was I a musician, too?

No, a collage artist. Was there anything someone could see? Not yet, maybe later. I worked with paper and text. I positioned things, then smoothed them out. Ancient history, Japanese poetry. I thought about using gold paint, or silver. I remembered there was such a thing as an illuminated manuscript.

There are very few human beings who receive the truth, complete and staggering, by instant illumination. Most of them acquire it fragment by fragment, on a small scale, by successive developments, cellularly, like a laborious mosaic. (Anais Nin)

I consider taking a class in mosaic-making while you are stuck in bed. There is a class in which you create a self-portrait. You can work from a photograph or a mirror. It doesn't matter. You just have to bring plenty of things to break.

I consider taking a class in medieval manuscript techniques. There is a workshop that promises to teach students all the old skills. And then we will create some small illuminations based on our own designs. Unlike the workers in the Middle Ages who had no say in what to illustrate, who filled in the flourishes that had already been decided. Smoothing down the gold leaf using a dog's tooth. Monks had done this work in the past, but then demand increased, and workers in Rome and Paris were employed. They faced the same materials day after day. Never taking a vacation. Doing one thing well, forever.

I am thinking about things to do while you are unavailable. But I don't know how long things will take. I don't know how long you'll remain.

I tell everyone, when I have to tell the story all over again, that we were just ordinary New Yorkers on vacation in Venice. Looking for landmarks and distractions. I don't talk about being artists. No one needs to know about that. I say we were tourists. Trying to avoid the traps.

Were you scared of being trapped? Is that what happened? Were you tired of doing all the things I wanted to do that you didn't really like? Were you tired of buying me jewelry? Were you about to leave me right before you fell? Did you think you had to choose between love and songwriting? Did you feel, all of a sudden, that the constraints of life in our apartment were too great? Were you tired of your room that someone painted (was it me or you?) to look like the dark side of the moon? Were you unable to do what was necessary? Were you not composing what you wanted? You never said anything.

And then, on the steps, so slippery, some drizzle, and the smallest splinter of music, maybe opera, I have no idea, floating out of someone's window. While I was looking at the pink. A scrap of sky. A scrap of paper. Something I could use. Did you see it, too? Did that do it? Or was it something you heard? What made you turn around? Was it something I said? Your scarf was so long and dripping into a puddle. Did you trip? Is that what made me reach out, as if to grab you? I can't tell. But do you remember?

You fell, and I failed to catch you. I won't even try to describe to your mother what happened.

Your mother says I should bring objects for you. Something to comfort. Some souvenirs or something that might make you happy. They might make you think. They might make you change. I told her I've already tried some things. Also, they don't let me bring in any electronics.

Are you okay with nothing?

Also, how do I know which souvenirs you loved? They are not the same as mine, I suppose. That is, I know.

What about a work of art to hang up? Something to look at. I don't know.

What good is a work of art if it can't help you through a difficult situation? If you can't cling to it in an emergency, like a cushion for flotation?

I should have asked you before now what things you would take to a desert island. Which eight songs, what book, and one luxury?

Do you remember the souk and the snakes under baskets and the croissants in the cafes surrounding the maze of stalls, where we thought we might get lost, where we bought the cheap silver teapot that we kept forever but never used? We never drank tea, only coffee. But that wasn't in Venice, of course not.

The best croissants we ever had were in the subway station in Osaka.

How much do you remember about Japan? Should we have gone back to Japan when we had the chance? Would that have been better than Venice? Do you wish things had been different?

Maybe they were different. What do you remember? Can you spell it out for me? Or for them? The authorities are here now.

They want to ask you some questions. They want you to tell them all about it, blink by blink. What happened?

They tried to talk to you at the start, but you weren't helpful. They think you might be able to communicate now. Now that you've had some time to think about it. They have to make sense of some things. They have to write it down.

Don't worry, I've already told them: you are stubborn and unreliable. And the method is difficult. Like talking through a Ouija board. They say they've seen it all before.

I say that you might not say anything. You're not talking to people. You're not even talking to me, that is, not really.

We were in the middle of things when everything happened. We had work to do, and we were doing it. Things seemed to be working. We each had something. Even though your mother said everything was make-believe. What she meant was unbelievable. What she meant was unreasonable. Because we had both been something else once, but then we gave that up and started again, and we hoped for something else. We were still young, more or less, and we thought we could do something.

We made the switch. From being what we were to becoming this.

Your mother asked: How is that better than having children?

All over New York, in different galleries, I see collages using pieces of paper. There are grids and flurries. Squares and rectangles.

If you wait long enough, someone else will do exactly what you imagined.

My collages: I would like to describe them for you, what's happened, but they're so hard to describe. Just text and paper.

The trick is knowing how much to use. How many scraps before the whole thing turns to trash, to mush, like papier-mâché, almost. How much is enough?

Wasn't there someone who sang about how we can't get enough of? (Depeche Mode)

We were in the middle of things when we went to Paris. Also, Venice, yes. I told the authorities they could talk to me instead of you. I would tell them what I could. We were just tourists, on vacation. What did we do?

We traveled, we walked. I stopped. I liked to stop at stalls and shops and find magazines to read in languages I didn't understand. Do you remember magazines? And then I liked to tear out words in bright colors. Headlines about homes and clothes, how to cook dinner, how to make time for the things you love. I took whatever words looked beautiful. Words that could be reused.

While you liked to stay behind and get to work in a dark room, with blackout shades, if they were available. Headphones, if necessary. But then you liked to go out and listen. You wanted to make good use of whatever location we were in. That's what I like to tell people when they ask me some questions.

Maybe I shouldn't tell you this, but my collages are piling up. I can't explain it, the momentum. They take a lot of effort, but I'm doing more than ever. Although you never stopped me from doing anything. From do-

ing something. From having something to do every day.
I don't know what to say. Maybe I shouldn't have said
anything.

I would like to provide for you, but I know this is
not the way.

I come to this room and see you every day. It's for your
own good. I push open the heavy door. Why do they
keep closing it? Has anyone told you anything that will
help? Have you received any encouragement? I'm sorry. I try to touch your skin through the bandages but I
don't know if that's painful. It's impossible to tell what
you like. What is life like for you now? Are you all right?

I'm fine. But I'll need to rent a storage space soon. Put
some things away. Especially if you think we might
move back to London. We can't take everything with
us, not again. We could live nearer the Thames, that
might be nice. I hope you haven't forgotten about that.
Your job offer, another chance, one more time. And
what was that job offer about exactly? Never mind, it
doesn't matter. I could never understand what kind of
music they were paying you for. The things that people
want to listen to in another country.

You thought I could work in any city. Why not? My
work wasn't site-specific. Or so you thought. You said

I could get a room with a window, looking out over the river. I could take a pile of blank canvases with me. You always said we could do anything. You would do anything for me.

Although, really, moving to London isn't going to happen now, is it?

Do you remember the first time we tried it, when we thought everything would work out, when we were out looking for flats, and the estate agent showed us that crazy place with the tiny terrace that overlooked the cemetery where William Blake is buried? The space was too angled and cramped. But we liked the idea of the cemetery. A cup of tea on the terrace in the afternoon overlooking it. That would have been nice.

Now, when I walk over here in the afternoons, I walk through the oldest (almost) cemetery in Manhattan. I walk through the cemetery in order to avoid the tourists. It is always cool and dark on that path. A relief in this summer. There are no names that I recognize on the stones. The stones are so old, inscrutable. I mean, illegible. The portals of the church are crumbling, too. Don't worry, they will put up some scaffolding soon.

At least you don't need a nightlight in here. The city outside, seeping in, is enough. There is a woman across the street who puts a pink neon heart on her windowsill occasionally. I don't know what it means. I don't know who she is signaling. Do you?

It doesn't matter. But can you see it?

Someone outside is singing. It's that crazy person who sleeps on the corner. He knows all the good songs. He even has a microphone (unplugged) that he uses.

Should I sing you a song? No, I'm sorry, that's a terrible idea. You would hate that. I don't know what I was thinking. I was thinking about your mother. She says we need to try something new. Because this isn't working. But she doesn't know what to do.

Blink twice if you want me to continue.

I'll be back tomorrow, either way.

If I sang a song, would that make you want to sing along, even though that's impossible?

Every day is a failure. No progress, no reprieve.

Is that what I think or is that you?

I tried to tell the authorities that you wouldn't say anything. They want to reassure me that you're not under suspicion. You have nothing to lose. They just need to know what happened, in your own words. This is how they approach everyone. Your mother doesn't understand why you can't make the effort. She would also like for you to talk to her at some point. She is dying to ask you some questions. I told everyone to leave you alone. You need to rest. I don't know if they believed me. I forced them out of the room. I said they didn't understand what you've been through.

What I like about collage art is that everyone understands it. Because who hasn't had to pick up some pieces and think about things? And then the relief of a swath of color. An indulgence. The fantasy of form without content. That would be wonderful. Just a French phrase in pink. Everyone can take it or leave it.

Your mother says my collages are inconceivable. I think she means inconsequential.

And she doesn't understand your music.

I'm sorry, I wasn't paying attention. I was looking out of your window. Look at that: orange sky, teal river. Can you make anything of it from where you are? Can you even see it? Do you want me to reposition the bed?

Someone has put up a sign outside of a storefront that says: Become Your Dream. What do you think that means?

Are you comfortable?

Although I know that comfort isn't the most important thing in the world to you. Or rather, it wasn't. There was always something else. I can't remember what you called it.

Can you hear the hawks screeching outside? They are nesting at the top of that skyscraper across the street. Circle and repeat.

Can you hear the ice-cream truck going up the street?

I wish I could bring you some music. But it's not possible. Only books, which you don't want to read. Even so, I come here every day, with books and magazines. The magazines are for me. I know you think they're useless.

You know I come here every day, don't you?

What would happen if I accidentally fell down the longest flight of subway stairs in the city on my way over here one afternoon? What would you do then? Could you survive without me?

Or what if I fell onto the subway tracks? Because people die every year like that. Most of those deaths are suicides, I know that. I understand. But some of those subway deaths are accidents. Some are homicides. The subway announcements say to stand behind the yellow lines, but who does that?

I don't usually take the subway in the afternoons. I like to walk. See what's out there. I might find something I can use. I usually follow the same route. I know I should try a different way, take a look down the side streets, take my chances, but I am like a rat in a maze, and once I know where I'm going, I keep going, the same way.

If you look closely at the bottom of buildings, you can see a fine black line running through the bricks. This is the oil from rats' whiskers. They make a streak as they follow their path. From the trash cans to the luxury building basements. Always the same path, night after night. Because it's hard to break a habit. I read it in a magazine.

You know that I come to see you every day, every afternoon. Even on the days when you don't open your eyes. You can still hear me talk. Right? I come to this room every day. It doesn't matter what happens. The doctors say they can't say anything yet. They say it is not wrong for me to hope, however.

It doesn't matter what other things I'm doing. I come to this room every day.

When I'm not here, I work on my collages.

And I might take a class. Knitting or weaving. I wonder which way is better. I would like to make more of my own things. That would be great.

Your mother sometimes, not often, asks how I'm doing. She says she knows it's hard to live alone. I tell her I'm fine. I have plenty of things. Plenty of things to do. She says: Don't be ridiculous. Everyone needs someone else to talk to. I quote to her from my copy of *Death in Venice*, about how solitude gives birth to poetry.

Your mother says she doesn't understand how someone could read something like that, so stupid. And what kind of person would write that down? For future reference.

Do you remember when we were in Athens? With the golden dust. Sand in the streets.

And then the beach. Two men on lounge chairs. One had a cane; the other was tan. One of them was much older, but it was hard to tell which. Too much sun. One said something about Venice. Maybe we should go back? But the other one didn't answer. He spoke a different language. Their hair was turning silver and gold. One said it was time to leave. But they were immobile, immobilized by something. They were two

statues, stones on the beach. They appeared to be holding hands. Neither one got up to go, even after the sun
sank and turned green at the last moment.

You fall asleep at every story I try to tell you. I know
it's difficult. Paying attention, pretending to care about
other people.

In the evenings, after dinner, I've been going through
our shelves, looking at all the old books, everything
I've saved, looking for clues, that is, comfort. Someone
must have written something.

I read in a book about a condolence note that Hemingway wrote to his friends when their son died, in which
he said that the child had now gone and done what
everyone must. I don't know if anyone found comfort
in that, in the sun, on the beach, in the south of France.
Maybe someone did, somewhat.

Do you remember Hemingway's house in Key West?
With his books on the shelves.

   Heads of animals on the walls, one black typewriter,
and a stuffed miniature black bull on the bookcase,
which at first seemed silly, but.

   I remember those bullfights. Would you like to see

one? I mean again, more than once? Or is that the last thing you want in this life?

I remember the books about bullfighting. The matador, alone on the page. Everyone making a spectacle of himself.

But I know you never read them.

I read a magazine article about a Japanese architect who created a house for a couple who had a lot of books. He created a slot in the wall to hold one book, carefully selected from their collection, one book that would represent all the others. The other books would have to be donated to charity.

I could write you a book. No, not really, but I could write you a letter. That's something. But I'm not going to do that, of course not. Because then you would have to read it, which you wouldn't like, and then you would have to respond to it, which would be terrible.

I continue to work while you're stuck in here. Your mother asks how I am doing it. What is the purpose of all these scraps? Am I making a scrapbook? Or something like that.

I pretend not to hear her. I continue. To put together the things I have, the things I find. I like to think it's going somewhere. I like to think that I am. That I will arrive at the final destination, the grand finale, like floating into the Grand Canal at sunset, somehow. But it/I might just be going in circles. I can't tell until it's finished, and I can step away and look back on something, as if it were a mandala. As if I were on top of a skyscraper, looking down. Can you hear me? Do you understand?

Your mother says an education has been wasted on me. She means that I wasted my education. What she means is that I'm taking advantage of you. How long have I been calling myself an artist? Your mother says an artist is someone in a museum. She doesn't mean a tourist.

It might be nice to work in pinks and bronze. Great streaks over large canvases. But, obviously, I don't have the temperament for that kind of work. I need something more portable. Ivory paper. Or mulberry. Putting words on paper: there is always more work like that.

But I do more than work on collages. I also do all the other things around the apartment, as always, as before, so that nothing falls apart. I polish the faucets and wash the walls where the dogs rub against the corners. I compose vignettes on the occasional tables. There are plenty of things to be done on a daily basis. I can't help it. I could not, as you did, ignore everything else in the apartment, in order to write music. Of course, I don't write music. I never did. I never would. Don't worry about that. I never could.

You didn't care about our apartment or the neighborhood. You could live anywhere. New York or London, what's the difference? Who cares if things are a mess? There was always the music. What a relief. I said something else. But we didn't fight about it.

When I walk down Thames Street in New York, I remember that we used to live in London. And England is an island, just like Manhattan, or close enough.

Your mother said that whatever I am telling you is disconnected from reality. But you don't have to believe that.

I always thought that if I were in your situation, with my life upended, that I would panic. Struggle to get back, to get out. Struggle to get better. But maybe not.

Maybe you are doing your best. Are you thinking of Keats, dying of tuberculosis, with so little time left? I don't know if you ever think about Keats. I don't know what you've read.

Keats is buried in the same cemetery as Shelley in Rome. Do you remember the stones? Shelley's grave has that quote from *The Tempest*. Gregory Corso is buried there also. So many plots, very close together.

I walk through the cemetery on my way over here in the afternoons. Sometimes, the tourists are there with crayons and paper, making rubbings of the ornaments on headstones.

I'm sorry, maybe I shouldn't talk about cemeteries. I should tell you something else, something better. What do you want to hear? I could try to entertain you. But you never wanted entertainment, not really. There was something else. All you ever wanted was a certain kind of music that I can't even describe. Much less provide.

I sometimes take my time on my way over here.

I stop at the deli and buy flowers.

I look in other people's windows, wherever there is a chandelier.

I think of what I'm going to say when I get here.

Should I tell you about my work or my life?

Wasn't there someone who sang about how every day, every day? (Elvis Costello)

There was a blue plaque on the yellow bricks of an old building on St. Thomas Street, marking where Keats lived for a while in London. I don't know if you remember it. I used to walk by his plaque every day, although you didn't. You stayed at home in your room like a tomb. Your songs were so soft and quiet that the neighbors never complained. Your music was like velvet, although I know that's not what you'd call it. I read in a magazine that some people in New York actually like to live next to musicians—for the free soundtrack to city living.

Do you remember how every house was a tomb in Pompeii?

The tour guide talked about the artists who lived there, the painters. How the painters who lived there burned bone or ivory, depending on what they had, when they needed black for their art. They knew what they had to do.

But maybe no one meant to keep any of those wall paintings and small paintings and all the other things in the museum (perfume bottles, wine jugs, rouge gone black in a scallop shell), all those things filling up the glass cases. Maybe all of that would have gone out of style and been destroyed or erased or recycled and we would have never had to spend hours in the museum in Naples thinking about beauty, materials, dreams. We would have never had to do anything.

When we went to Venice, we were both working on something. Something different.

We were always going somewhere. I liked to say I was looking for inspiration. You always said you didn't care.

When we went away, someone came and sat with the dogs. Your mother couldn't believe that was someone's job.

We went out of town often. Lisbon, Islamorada, Saigon.

The cemeteries in Paris were so— Also London.

But Keats is buried in Rome. Do you remember when we went to find his grave? All those cats and the smell of coffee from cafes. The smell of croissants, although they called them something else.

Your mother said we were crazy. Why couldn't we stay in one place like normal people? She hadn't moved across the world to bring you to this country in order for you to grow up and leave it. She wished you could have achievements like the children of people who were her friends.

Your mother says I shouldn't talk about cemeteries in front of you. Bad luck.

Your mother says I don't know what I'm talking about. But how does she know that?

Walking over here to see you this afternoon, after coming out of the cemetery, I saw the snakes were out again in front of Federal Hall for the summer. They sit curled up in their baskets. Tourists stop. Men charge money if you want to take a picture. They are pythons, I think. Escaped from Florida. There are alligators in the subways.

No, I'm only joking.

The streets are like a swamp today and city feels tropical. Or subtropical, rather. There are people with sticky plastic bags full of papayas.

Do you remember St. Lucia? How we drove all around that island in order to find the best, tenderest conch? I had to have it. And you would do anything for me. Those were the days. You never complained, even when you thought I was crazy. And we found it, the restaurant with a big pink sunset sign out front. But when I tried to order conch, the waitress apologized. None today.

This had happened to me before, more than once.

Disappointment all over the Caribbean.

Conch is always hand-written on the daily menu, regardless of availability.

Spend your money on travel and experiences. I read it in a magazine. This is how to achieve happiness. Spend whatever you've got on extravagant dinners and nights filled with music. Trips through Morocco and Iceland and Japan. Spend it on things you can look forward to, then look back on later. Because these things will provide pleasure forever.

We had enough money, so why were we still trying to create something? That's what your mother wanted to know. What was the purpose of art if I didn't show it? Why were you so anonymous? Do you remember what we told her?

I still have all the conch shells we took from all the different islands. You could never resist a perfect shell. The sound it made. They are still lined up on a shelf in your room. I haven't dismantled that, not yet.

You always liked music so quiet that it was almost silent. Subtle is what you called it. Music like gauze.

Something to surround you, a cocoon. Something to keep you safe. You said music should speak for itself. And then when it's gone, that's okay, move on to something else. Your music was refined. Everyone said the same thing.

My work was rougher, cobbled together.

We made a good couple. That's what I thought. That's what I said.

I've had to rent a storage unit for my canvases. The collages are getting larger, bolder, and I am using more color. But mostly they've increased in volume. They are too much for our apartment. Things are piling up. It's hard to see clearly anymore. I can't think about how to proceed, how to progress. I might have to find a larger space.

I walk down the street, carrying one big square at a time. And then I go back home. I thought you should know how far I've come, how far gone.

You never understood my work but you never tried to stop me.

On the street, earlier today, I watched two men in mango ties take a break at lunchtime to sit in front of a skyscraper, on its steps. They blew smoke into the air. The money, one said, is the main thing.

Long ago, when we first started, before you made any money, before I had any art, there was a small hotel on Tortola, do you remember it? The water from the faucet was brown. The ocean was full of kelp. We sat out on the sand at five o'clock in the afternoon. I picked up pieces of coral from the seaweed. What to do with them? White sails made circles around islands. You listened to the ocean. We sat among the ghost crabs. Do you remember this? Do you remember that? Does it help if I tell you, if I spell it out? The breeze blew apart a few hot pink fantasy streaks of sunset. We did nothing, for a long time. We looked at the clouds. Which turned black. Everything could have ended there, that night. And we didn't do anything about it.

There is a cloud appreciation society whose members are committed to looking at clouds and enjoying life. They don't have to talk about what they see, necessarily. That's what I read in a magazine.

The situation is the same as before. No electronics in this room. Maybe later. I'm sorry. In the meantime, just being here every day, doing my best: that's enough, that's what they said. They said you appreciate it. I don't know how they can tell.

Is my presence a comfort or a torment?

Your mother and I have split the day into shifts. It's best if we don't overlap too much. She wants to know why I couldn't be the one confined to a bed, unable to talk, unable to move, instead of you. My life reduced to a series of blinks. Why wasn't I the one who fell down the steps? That would have been so much better.

I was the one who suggested we take off to Paris, at a moment's notice. Then Budapest, even Venice.

What should we do next? We went to Venice to find out.

We liked to get away. That's what we always said. We could talk about moving to London later. We didn't need to make a decision right away. We didn't even tell your mother about our itinerary.

When you fell down the steps, my life also fell apart. Or is about to.

We were just tourists, doing the most obvious things. We played along. But we also did something else. We still do.

That is, do you? Are you still writing music? Without writing it down, that is. Are you thinking about it? Or something like it?

I know you liked to say music should dissolve, as
if written in invisible ink, but you don't want it to be
erased entirely, do you? Or do you?

You should tell me what I can do.

I don't remember what it was that made us run, in the
rain, over various bridges, down those steps.

Someone needed to go, to make a move. Who?

You were wearing that incredibly long striped scarf,
which was a mistake. And then there was thunder,
which made us jump. I think.

The storm has washed the streets clean this afternoon.
People like black flies have been pushed aside. The
green plastic bags have been blown out to sea. Can you
see the water through the window? Giant cruise ships
slip between the gaps in skyscrapers. Helicopters take
tourists up and down the edges of Manhattan. Even
though one malfunctioned yesterday and fell out of the
sky and someone died.

Marble steps in the rain are the smoothest thing. Slippery when wet. No running. That's what people said.

Are you listening? Sometimes you ignore me, as if I

were an annoyance. As if you have something better to do. As if I were your mother.

But this is how you've always been. I learned to live with it.

I used to ask you questions and you pretended not to hear them. How was your day? What did you do? Can you play something new for me on the piano? Did you see the news? What do you want for dinner? Cod? Chicken? Chorizo?

Sometimes, I would call out to you in your blue room and wait for an answer. I would wait a few minutes, and then, if nothing, I would make up an answer for you. Pretend that I knew.

You used to hate all the questions. Do you still? I know that's why you loved music. That's what you said. But was it true?

And how would you like me to communicate? How else to proceed? What do you want me to do?

I found *The Gift of Death* (Derrida) on your shelf by our bed in the apartment. It said: "We are given over to absolute solitude. No one can speak with us and no one can speak for us; we must take it upon ourselves, each of us must take it upon himself."

You weren't reading that, were you? Because that was my book.

I don't even know what you were composing when all of this happened. Was there an Italian allusion? The infusion of something Venetian? You never let me hear it, whatever it was. You never explained it. Was it too much? Or just unfinished?

You always said music was a process of elimination. So much noise in the world, especially New York, and you were trying to reduce it, down to something, not necessarily beautiful, but something else, yes. I always said the opposite, that art was a process of accumulation. We went to work in our separate rooms every day. The dogs would split up, too, one in each room.

We never talked about what we had to do. And then you went out, with your equipment, and then you came back to your room before dinner.

Your room was dark and quiet, painted in a color called Sea of Tranquility, but mine had a window that tourists passed under. They clustered and clumped in colors like raspberry and peach. I never wanted to talk to them, not for one minute.

How should we live with art in our lives? That's the kind of question I liked to ask you, the kind of question you refused. But how would we survive? That is, should I get a job?

Do you want to see some pictures of paintings? I just thought of that. Maybe it would help. I can't tell. There's an exhibition of Klimt's paintings in town. I can bring you the catalog. I read about the exhibit in a magazine. You can look at that woman in that gold painting. She lived in a gilded cage, supposedly, because she couldn't do anything, not really, in Vienna, not then.

But we've already seen this painting, I hope you can remember that. And then we ate wiener schnitzel in the cold with a cold potato salad.

The streets are so empty this afternoon. Only snow. Not even an occasional streak of taxi yellow. I walked all the way over here. The delis have no roses. The wind whistles through the spaces between buildings, through the buildings, even. The river is almost frozen. Your mother asks if my heater is working. She says hers makes too much noise. The banging is driving her crazy. Can you believe living in this world? I'm sorry. I tell her my heater is quiet. Or rather, I don't notice it.

There are other things I could tell you. What would you like to hear? Your face is like a mask. Are you happy? Are you worried? What are you trying to accomplish?

These are the same questions your mother used to ask. I remember how you ignored her.

What's going to happen if you never finish what you started? If you never get to do what you always wanted? Because you know I can't do it for you. I don't understand music at all. I don't even know the words you use for it.

What about what you've already done? Is it enough? I don't know. Try not to think about your life chronologically for one moment.

After I leave you and go home, every night, I make dinner, as if you were still alive. I mean, available, about to come out of your dark room with the headphones on. Or maybe you were out in the city, doing whatever work you had to do that day. What were you trying to record? The sounds of mermaids on Coney Island? I don't know.

I make stuffed poblanos, shrimp curry, and coq au vin, among other things. I use all my cookbooks. I make recipes that serve four to six people. That way, I have leftovers.

After dinner, in the evenings, I read and work. Tearing up paper, looking for words. Putting words onto paper, and paper on canvas. Then I seal everything in. My pieces are minimal, but my production is increasing.

I feel like I have all the time in the world. To do what?

After dinner, in the evenings, I walk the dogs, back and forth.

Didn't you once say it would be great to have a serious but not deadly illness so that one could stay in bed all day and do some good work? Compose a song. Compose a life. Or maybe I was the one who said that. Or I might have read it somewhere. I can't remember. But here you are.

I don't know how long you can stay here like this. Your mother says her money is running out. She has been paying for things, extras. I don't know what she's talking about. I told her that was crazy. She shouldn't be using her money like that. Plus, we have enough money for everything. Right?

Although, eventually, our money will run out, too, I guess. Yes? Maybe sooner than expected. What do you think? The doctors say you can't stay here forever.

What will I do when that happens? What will I do without you?

They have returned to ask you some questions, to try again. The authorities. From several divisions. They have pulled out their notebooks and flipped through them. No recording devices are allowed in this room.

They ask you questions and you don't blink. They don't know what to do. Because there's nothing they can do to you. Nothing they can do for you either. They are stuck.

So why won't you tell them the truth?

Would you like to stay here forever, just like that, serene inside your skin and bandages, happy in the blue behind your eyelids? But I'm not going to ask you that.

You can tell me the truth. Did you do it on purpose? That fall down the steps, that's what I'm talking about.

Did you decide to choose something else? And then this is what you got instead?

Is it too much effort to answer these questions?

Yes, that's what I've told the authorities. You need to rest.

They have left to figure it out.

Is it too much for you? Even when you're alone with me? Because it's just me and you now, you can see that, right?

Are you looking out of the window?

Are you lazy? Are you crazy?

What else do you have to do?

Are you trying to live your life? Are you writing songs?

Do you want me to leave now?

I'll be back tomorrow. Don't worry.

I read in a magazine that there will be times in your life when you're trapped—in the waiting room, stuck in an elevator—and you'll be glad to have memorized some poems. The words will help you get through certain situations. I suppose song lyrics will work just as well.

Even if the lyrics are stripped of the music?

Have you memorized anything? Were you thinking ahead? Is it too late?

Snow is predicted for the whole week. Although I know you don't care about the forecast, you never did. It doesn't matter what the weather is.

Also, there is snow on the ground already. Fireplaces are glowing in tiny restaurants. People are wrapped up. I saw a dog walk by in a mink coat.

Be careful not to slip on black ice. Be careful when traveling out of the country. Men are more likely than women to die from injuries abroad. Men are more reckless. That's what I read in a magazine. That's what the Centers for Disease Control said.

Those polished marble steps were so steep in Venice. The slide down so easy. I was surprised to see you slipping, almost sweepingly. As if you had flung yourself.

I reached out but I didn't push you away. That's what I think.

The authorities want to ask you some questions in order to be sure it was an accident. They have to make some recommendations, going forward, about money and things, compensation. I don't think they suspect anything.

If you did it on purpose, it doesn't make any sense. Because it would have been easier in Nara, at the white castle with those narrow wooden steps like a ladder. Do you remember? You were looking at the long, smooth walls with secret panels while climbing up. I imagine you were imagining where the ninjas were hiding. Or rather where they were hidden, long ago. Back when no one suspected something would jump out from nothing.

We fell in love with Japan. I always thought we would go

back. Although there was something about the music I
didn't understand. Was it traditional or minimal? Do
you remember? I let you have the music while I looked
at the folded paper and the flower arrangements. At the
rocks in gardens.

Do you remember the rock garden in Kyoto? The one
with fifteen stones. Laid out in such a way that only
fourteen are visible from any point on the viewing
porch. Fifteen is a number that signifies perfection,
completion, and so, ideally, you should see all fifteen in
one glance. Wasn't that the story they were telling us?
But given the conditions of human existence, a view of
all fifteen stones is not possible. Pick and choose. We
kept walking, back and forth across the viewing porch.
The wood felt like lacquer. We tried to see everything
all at once.

In Tokyo, you went to find the singing bowls, while I
looked at the raku glazes on cups.

I thought I would take a class, back in New York, about
how to mend broken Japanese ceramics with golden
lacquer. You fill in the cracks so that the piece is more
valuable than before, when it was whole, but I don't
know.

I have to go home now. I'll be back tomorrow.

The subway steps have iced over. They are as slick as river stones. Be careful.

Japanese tourists become delusional, anxious, and dizzy in Paris. They are especially susceptible to the Paris Syndrome, that's what I read in a magazine. It's because of the romantic image of Paris in Japanese advertising. Paris seems so beautiful. It makes them sing and swoon. They are overcome. And it doesn't even have to be April. Even in winter, they are undone.

Your mother said this winter will never end. She said this is a season not to be enjoyed. She is unhappy and tired of living alone. That's what she tells me in the hallway. She has no hobbies and no novels. I tell her I have to go home and walk the dogs. I tell her to get a dog. But she wants someone to talk to. I tell her she can talk to a dog all day, no problem. But a dog won't talk back, she says. I ask her why she needs someone to respond.

I tell your mother she should listen to the radio. There are so many stations. Any kind of music is available. You wouldn't believe the choices. Just pick something.

Your mother says listening to the radio is a waste of time. Reading novels, also. And magazines! She says you should be doing something with your life instead. Something great. Something grand. She means me, not you.

Is that saxophone on the corner driving you crazy? I will try to get rid of it. See if I can close the window. Plus, the tourists will be coming down this street any minute.

How could you ever hear anything with headphones on in this city? I was always afraid you'd get yourself killed. There were so many tourists, and they didn't know what they were doing. They didn't know where to look. How to walk. When to keep up. And what if someone came up behind you? What if a bus turned a corner too fast? When you wore those headphones, do you remember how you could never hear anything I asked? I never used headphones, even on a plane. I used to watch other people's video screens without any sound of my own. The last thing I saw was a shark video, all blood and water, at a resort on an island that we were headed toward.

Your bandages look better today. White as marble,

maybe. Did someone rub a balm over your skin? Did you get any sleep? Can you smell the croissants from the bakery across the street?

Do you remember when we stayed in that white chateau outside of Paris? With the wind through the forest and leaves blowing across the patio. You liked the sound of that. I'm sure you remember because it wasn't so long ago. We arrived late, drank red wine, went to sleep. Until pounding music started at midnight. Where was it coming from? We called the front desk. They would check. In the morning, the music stopped and we were told: a rave in the forest. The police had been looking for them all night, but they were smart: no lights. Only music in the dark. Hidden until morning, when they escaped. Or rather, departed.

I read in a magazine that one surefire way to make yourself happier is to listen to music, even sad music, it doesn't matter. I wonder if the same is true for words. Does reading always work?

Your mother tells me that reading is not a cure for loneliness. Neither is listening to music. Or cooking dinner. Or knitting. Or gibberish. That's what she calls my collages. I think she means pastiche.

I can't believe they won't let you have any devices in here. Because you're not a prisoner. I can't believe they won't let you have this one thing that means the world to you.

I'm sorry. I don't know how long this will go on. The doctors say they can't predict the future.

Because we don't know when we will die, we get to think of life as an inexhaustible well. Yet everything happens only a certain number of times, and a very small number really…. How many more times will you watch the full moon rise? Perhaps twenty. (Paul Bowles)

The Sea of Tranquility: wasn't that the title of a piece of music? Was it something you composed? Or was it someone else? I would play it for you, if I could.

Are you composing in your head right now some sort of music that you will never share? Do you compose nonstop? This is what you always wanted, isn't it? Art for one. Is that even possible? What does that involve and will it have been worth it? And what will it be when it's finished? Who can tell.

But what if you never finish what you started? Are you going to keep going, regardless?

As for me, my collages, I'll have to stop eventually. They can't go on forever, I know that. There isn't enough space inside our apartment.

There isn't enough text. There isn't enough glue.

Your mother said my work was a mishmash. I hope she meant montage.

Do you remember walking along the river in Budapest? When the sun hit the water, which turned to gold. A castle in the distance. A bit of American music escaped from an open city window and you remembered something, all of a sudden. You could sing along even though you hadn't heard that song in years. I mean, I was the one singing, until you told me to stop.

When you tripped and fell, did you think that might be the end? I have to believe you never imagined all this, the room, the bandages, the frozenness, the partial views of New York City. Did you do it on purpose? Were you trying to escape? Did you feel it was a chance you had to take? Do you remember anything? Do you think it might have been me who pushed you over the edge?

I read in a magazine that remembering something changes it. Changes the memory, that is. The more you remember it, the less likely it is to be like the original.

There's just too much information for the brain to retain everything. So memories shift, disappear, re-emerge, accumulate, and then, in the end, mean something different.

Remembering something is like taking a trip. The destination turns out to be not what you expected at the beginning. It is not like what you planned, what you dreamed. So, what I'm saying is: Do you want to tell me anything? About your memories, your dreams? But you were never overcome by nostalgia, I know that. No use looking back. You were always thinking ahead. Paying attention. It's almost unbelievable that you fell the way you did. And in Venice, of all places.

We always came back to New York. This is where we did our work. The other places were extra, extraneous. In New York, we were artists, not tourists. I suppose we still are. That's what I tell people.

It's hard to remember/desire/decipher fragments of odd handwriting stuck together with the tiniest pieces of tape. There is an exhibit of Sappho fragments in Midtown. At the museum in the middle of summer:

ancient history and then some paper, paintings, peeling. People struggle to mind the gaps, to find them, to fill them in. Do you know who Sappho is? Read the writing on the wall. The captions in the catalog. Fish some pages out of the trash. The Parthenon on a paper cup. Cold coffee. Think of the glamour of travel and where to go now. Would you like to see the ruins or the islands?

You always liked to go to an island and sit in a cool, dark room with palm fronds and overhead fans. I liked to sit on the sand and sift for shells, stones. The best ones had a tiny hole for a string.

Walking over here this afternoon, I heard someone say to someone else: She was just trying to get to a better place. They were looking up at a fire escape.

But that's someone else's life. I don't know whose. I know you don't care.

Remember when you used to tune me out? Sometimes, you even wore your headphones inside the apartment. But I understood: there was always work to do, and you worked when you had to. You heard something I couldn't. There was music that had to be captured. I knew what you had to do. Don't worry about that.

Are you keeping a record of the things I say to you?
Does it sound like the story of your life? Is anything
helping? Is anything helpful? Are you making a recording inside your head? Do you repeat the things I've
told you when I leave the room? Can you still hear me?
Blink twice for yes.

You know you can talk to me about anything. Any
fantasies? Any regrets? What do you want? I know
you're in an impossible situation, but still, there must
be something.

How will I know when you stop listening?

Would you like me to reposition the bed so that you can
have a better view of outside? I have been looking out
of that window all this time. I'm sorry. I don't know
what I was thinking. I should have made sure you could
see the same thing.

But I thought you'd rather stare at the alphabet
chart. How many blinks for each letter. But now I
know better.

Such a simple city window. But open to interpreta-
tion. I have opened it for you now, that's all I'm saying.

The sky outside is some sort of slate gray. Can you see
it now? Sometimes there's music. Can you hear it? I

know that an opera singer lives across the street. She
always opens her window at twilight. To serenade the
sidewalk. She must drive her neighbors crazy.

An opera singer used to live below us. Do you remember? Her singing sometimes sounded like the wind
coming around the street corners in winter. I didn't
even realize it was music until you told me.

How many opera singers are there in this city?

You kept your headphones on, even in the apartment,
in your dark blue room, before dinner. I cooked while
dogs barked. And then we all ate together, around our
round table. And then you would go back to work. Later, we would walk together sometimes, talk together.
Sometimes not. I tried to work on my collages.

You might think it's fine if you stay here, in this
high, white, blank bed. Like a butterfly in a shadow-
box. Pinned, fixed. But you have to snap out of this
eventually.

We're paying a lot for all of this. Your life-insurance
policy doesn't kick in unless you actually die. I'm sorry.
What I mean is that we never made arrangements for
this kind of situation. Although it was offered to us:
insurance against decay, disaster, disintegration. We
didn't take it.

The doctors say you can't stay here forever. Do you know what I'm saying?

Your mother would say the same thing, if she were able.

The authorities have returned. I had forgotten about them. While you've been ignoring them. Either way. They still have the same questions.

This time, it's a different team determined to make progress. They want to talk to you about your life and/or insurance plan. They wonder if you might be a victim. Although they didn't say that, not quite. They want you to tell your side of the story. Bit by bit. However you have to do it. Blink by blink.

But you don't have to say anything, of course not.

They don't understand. Why you don't explain yourself. They ask me to reposition the bed so that you can see the alphabet chart. I tell them that won't change anything.

Your mother is trying to be helpful. She is telling them about your childhood. Nothing useful. They are not even writing it down.

They tell me that I have to talk to you. To explain that you have to talk to them. I tell them I don't see why or when. They say they are not in a hurry. They will take a break, come back later. Maybe tomorrow. Maybe I can convince you that other people will benefit from whatever you have to say here. Your story could be something. That's what they tell me to tell you. Okay?

You are in the perfect position to write a book. Everyone would read it. People would die to know how you survive all of this.

It would be difficult, of course. It would take everything you've got. Like composing a song. That's what I assume, although as you know, what do I know about creating a piece of music? But you could do it, if you wanted to. It might do you good. To have something to do. I could help you. But I can't tell you what to say.

But maybe no one is going to allow you to stay in here long enough to come up with the right thing anyway.

Music makes me forget myself, my true condition, it carries me off into another state of being, one that isn't my own: under the influence of music I have the illusion of feeling things I don't really feel, of understanding things I don't understand. (Tolstoy)

I copied that out for you. I can tape it to your wall if you want. Do you like it?

The paint on your wall is peeling, just a little bit. Have you noticed? I don't think it was like that when we started. The old magazines are falling apart. The new magazines are thin, useless.

The seasons have changed, maybe more than once. I should have paid attention, but I have other things to think about.

Why are there no mirrors in here? Has it always been like that? Can you remember? Maybe it's so you can't see what's happening. Maybe it's for the best. Also no clocks, just like a casino.

I hope I am a comfort to you. I don't want to reveal/reflect any terror. I try to keep the news out of this room, but who knows what your mother tells you.
You are like an iceberg. I will try to find a nurse.

Are you getting smaller?

Are you withering while I am not? I'm sorry.

Were you even listening to me when everything happened? Was it something I said on the steps that distracted you? You had a scarf wrapped around your neck, so long that it was trailing through the puddles. If you hadn't turned around, slightly, twisting just the wrong thing. If you hadn't thought I wasn't on your side. I'm sorry.

Regret is a useless emotion. I read it in a magazine. People begin to wallow in it and can't get out. I'm not sure why. Because of course things could have gone differently. They could have gone wrong long before that night.

Either you will wake up and tell the truth or I will walk out, when the time comes, and collect the insurance money. Assuming they don't suspect you of something. Or me, of something else.

I could live a long time on that money, even in the middle of New York City. But how much time do I need? I'm talking about my collages now, talking about them again. I have created so many collages already. Do you think I should try something else? I'm sorry. I shouldn't ask you these questions when you can't even come up with a song in the middle of your bed like a desert. But I am thinking ahead. To the next piece, what I might make, how to move on to something else. Sometimes, I add things to my text. Sometimes, text on text. Is that crazy to obscure one thing with something else? There's a word for that, I think. I mean, I know there is.

Your mother says she wishes you had a better life. She wants things to add up to something. Something greater than what we've got. She means she wishes you had a better wife.

I could live a long time on that money, even in the middle of New York City. Do you think people would think it's suspicious? If I continue to buy yellow roses in winter? What about black pearls? What if I stay put in our apartment, with two dogs, and continue to do my work? I could try to arrange it so that no one sees what I'm doing through the open windows.

I remember a necklace of pink glass beads in Venice. But that doesn't matter now, that's not what I want to talk about. Why were we even in Venice, can you remember? Can you tell me that much, at least? It was autumn, wasn't it, when we went. We'd been before, of course. But there were plenty of things we could do more than once. We could go to Venice every year, if we wanted to. If that's the place I wanted to pick.

But I keep thinking about that castle in Nara, how that would have been more suitable.

People fall down the stairs in Japan all the time. That's what I read. All that slick wood with white socks. Something could have happened there, and it wouldn't have been a problem.

Be true to the thought of the moment and avoid distraction. Other than continuing to exert yourself, enter into nothing else, but go to the extent of living single thought by single thought. (*Hagakure: The Book of the Samurai*)

Samurai used to imagine all the horrible things that could happen to them, as part of their training. That's what I read. They would envision all the ways they could fail. In order to be prepared for the day ahead, for whatever happened next.

I was not prepared for what happened next, now. I thought you would help me. I thought we were in this together, close enough, more or less. In any case, I didn't think I would be interrogated, but here I am. Answering questions.

2

Can you hear me?

Of course.

Everything is being recorded.

Okay.

We don't need your consent.

I'm sorry, I wasn't thinking. I was looking out of the window. Down the street. Steam is coming up from a vent. There are people wrapped up out there, wrapped up in things, and carrying cups of coffee. They have no idea what's happening in here.

It doesn't matter what they're doing on the sidewalk.

Can you tell us what happened? In your own words, nothing fancy.

I don't know if I can explain it. I don't know if I can explain myself, if that's what you're asking. And don't you know everything already?

We need to hear it again, one more time. It looks like you're going to have to answer some questions if you want to continue with what you have here.

There was an accident. While traveling. We were just tourists. Things crumble. People fall down. We were looking for landmarks. There were distractions.

We're going to need more than that.

I'm sorry, but we ran, if you want to know the truth. And someone got hurt.

What else?

I don't know. What?

It's getting late.

It's getting dark, I can see that, and I need to get back. I have things. How long will this last? How long will this take? The door seems to be locked. At least there's a window.

At least the blackout shades haven't been pulled down, not now, maybe later.

Can you speak louder, please? We need to be able to capture whatever is—

Where is my mother-in-law?

In the hall, talking to another agent. She remembers something, and she wants to talk about it.

Life is not what one lived but what one remembers. (Gabriel García Márquez)

I can't remember how we got here, how we got back here, with my husband, such a burden. Was it my mother-in-law who arranged everything? The flights, the right doctors. I might have been unable.

But that's at the end. What about the beginning?

Do you mean Venice?

Isn't that where your husband fell?

There were some steps and a bridge. Those steps were so slippery. It might have been raining, that's what I'm thinking. Those steps were marble, wet, white as milk.

But this condition he's in, that's not what usually happens to people. Most people would be dead. You're lucky you weren't detained. They could have kept you. Your husband is lucky, too.

They say he's stuck.

There was a palazzo apartment that we'd rented, and we had it for the whole month, although who knew if we'd keep it. We'd had an argument, something small, about art and love, love and work, I can't recall. But we needed to get out. Of the apartment, I mean. We were going to enjoy the evening as much as possible, then dinner. You have to eat. So that's where we were going, that's where we were headed. Risotto and clams, or something like that. It might have been Friday. There was running. Puddles and gutters. Pink streaks. I was wearing a necklace of glass beads.

Was your husband clumsy? Did he fall down a lot?

No, not at all.

Most people would be dead after a fall like that.

The doctor says we don't know if the fall caused his problem or if there was something that precipitated the fall.

Does anyone really need to run in a city like that? What for and how far?

I thought we were going to take a walk. Through the twilight. A romantic restaurant around the corner. I'd read all about it. Maybe it was the rain that made us run. Did we even eat dinner? We didn't want to get caught. We were just tourists.

The steps were so slippery. But it was my fault, I'll admit it. That we were in Venice at all. I'm sorry I'm so unoriginal.

And you planned to be there for an entire month? How was that going to work? Did your husband have a job? Who was making money?

He was a composer, of a sort. I don't know what kind of composer. I mean, I don't know what you'd call it. How many kinds are there? He never wrote lyrics, I know that much. I don't know anything about music, except what I hear on the radio.

And you say you're some kind of artist?

I like to find things, preserve things, prepare, and pin things down.

Taxidermy?

No.

I'm not sure I understand.

I can show you a picture.

Even the most perfect reproduction of a work of art is lacking in one element: its presence in time and space, its unique existence at the place where it happens to be. (Walter Benjamin)

Do you have access to your husband's work?

No, I'm sorry.

Your mother-in-law told us that you know his passwords. Or you can figure them out. Because there might be someone who wants to hear what he was working on, someone he was working for. There might be something someone can use.

But my mother-in-law doesn't know anything about music.

Is it true that your mother-in-law warned you not to go on this particular trip?

Yes, but she always said that. She was worried that something horrible would happen. This is her worst-case scenario, for example.

And where else did you go?

Over the years or just that one trip?

Either way.

Japan and Paris and Vienna. Other places as well. It will take me a while to remember all the names. We spent one season going to the bullfights in the ancient arenas. I remember the sand, such an expanse. Triumph seemed possible.

We were just tourists. Looking for landmarks and souvenirs. The best croissants. What happened in Venice was an accident. I don't know what else to tell you. People have accidents on vacation all the time. Car crashes, smoke inhalation, slips, falls. And those steps were so slippery, some drizzle. I remember a bit of music, maybe opera, I have no idea, floating out of someone's open window. One long striped scarf from a nice shop. My husband had just bought it. Puddles in the street and the end of our trip. I should have caught him when he fell. But I didn't, I couldn't. I saved myself.

My mother-in-law wouldn't understand that, so please don't say anything.

I remember some mummies in the British Museum. Wrinkled linen. A few faces streaked with gold. That gold was so thin.

How does this relate to that? You're talking about London now?

My husband had a job offer to move to London, where we had lived before. We had to talk about that at some point. We were going to talk about it in Venice, maybe, over dinner one evening, but we didn't.

My husband could write music anywhere in the world. He liked to write music anywhere in the world. Music was universal. No language necessary, no translation, do you know what I'm saying? But I didn't know if I could do my work outside of New York. So we had to talk about it. Whether we were going to move back. From one fantasy island to the next. Back and forth. But then he fell.

He might have been feeling trapped in New York, I don't know. Maybe he wanted to go back to London and try again. But he didn't say anything.

Let's try again tomorrow. You haven't told us anything that we didn't know already.

Things have gone grayer outside, I can see that now. Has something happened?

They tell me to go home and stay inside. Put on my hood when I exit the building. No contact with other people. No visits to your hospital room. They are keeping a log. They tell me to pretend I am in solitary confinement. But I have to walk the dogs! I ask them what you will do without me. They say you'll be fine. Nothing will change in my absence.

But I am not going to abandon you, don't worry. I read in a magazine that it's possible for things to affect each other across a great distance, things that have been entangled before. Even across the width of a universe. The article was talking about particles, not people. Even so. You know what I mean. Don't you?

And don't worry, the interrogators aren't going to get anything out of me, not really. They say don't forget that I'm not a prisoner. Just a little cooperation is all they need. A little confirmation. They want me to spell it out. Take it step by step. And then they will make a document.

I write differently from what I speak, I speak differently from what I think, I think differently from the way I ought to think, and so it all proceeds into deepest darkness. (Kafka)

I am reading books in the evening, rereading, going through our shelves, looking for answers. I wish I could find something to tell them.

Should I have been more systematic in the organization of our bookshelves? I could start again and sort everything by color. That would be something, wouldn't it? But there are very few books with yellow dust jackets in our apartment. Is that because very few are published?

In college, they told us there were two kinds of people who would do well, in classes, in life, forever: those who, as children, kept their crayons sharp and organized in boxes, and those who didn't care. Do you remember which kind of person you are? Venetian Red. Burnt Sienna.

I've been trying to remember what we were doing before all this. What had we been trying to do? What were we trying to prove? How long had you loved me, and did you still? Do you?

We were in the middle of things when everything happened. We had work, and we were doing it. But no one is going to ask me about that. About our art and what we thought. About what made us think we could.

The money: that's what they are worried about,

that's what they want to talk about, that's what it looks like, and that's what they are leading up to. We have to discuss money at some point, maybe tomorrow. I will have to explain what I can. As if I could. They are already suspicious. They already know what your life is worth. They have a calculation and a report. They already think I was taking advantage of you, that's what your mother suggested. Was it wrong to live in a palazzo in Venice while trying to create something?

Your mother said she wished our lives would add up to something. She thought the music you made for games was stupid. She never liked what I did, what I said, what I tried. Why did I need to take a class to learn how to gild paper? Was there anything more useless? She said that's the kind of question she would like to ask. And then she would like some answers.

We were always doing something. I remember how we used to work in different rooms, in hotels and apartments, it doesn't matter. I remember the windows and the streets. I remember walking down St. Thomas Street on my way to Borough Market every Friday afternoon in London. To buy fresh crab and Cumberland sausage. To cook just for you! The crab was so good in London, but where did it come from? You bought me cookbooks, and I used them. I loved those cookbooks. I still do. I made dinner in the evenings while you worked in your dark green room, south of the Thames. I took the room looking over the rose garden. Not our roses, of course not. Because we would have killed them.

I remember when we were living in London, when we had to get away. We went to Marrakesh. There was a souk and snakes under baskets and a cheap silver teapot that we kept forever but never used. We never drank tea, not really, not even when we were living in London. We also bought a tin of saffron that turned out to be colored thread.

The thread of a life is hard to break. I read it in a magazine. Private detectives can supposedly find you when you move to a different city because you keep doing the same things forever. You can't give up the old routines. The references and allusions. The things you try to tell people. The first editions of novels by Paul Bowles and Jane Bowles, too. The blue tagines and haiku manuals.

Maybe I shouldn't say anything, but the collages are piling up. I can't explain it, the momentum, I mean. Even though conditions aren't ideal. They are watching me. Do they think I will make a mistake? And I have to go into their room every day and answer too many questions, some of which I don't even understand, I'm sorry to say. So what are they trying to tell me?

But every day, I go in and tell them what I remember. Isn't it always the same thing? They say they appreciate my help. A cumulative effect. They say they are piecing it together. That it will all work out in the end. That it will be for the best. The final report will make sense. No one wants to stop too soon. That would not be acceptable. We have to see where this takes us. That's what they keep saying. As if I need to be persuaded.

They don't tell me anything about you, however. I ask them every day.

And, if you have lived a day, you have seen all: one day is equal and like to all other days. (Montaigne)

Is it a mistake to keep working on collages? Should I stop? Should I stop working? Would you call it struggling? Are those the only choices?

There are too many collages in the world already. I see them all over New York. Torn-paper compositions of scraps. Things encased, inlaid. Encaustic and resin. Does it look like the things I make? Don't worry, I'm trying to change. I am using more white space so that you can see the edges of everything. Like the spaces in a piece of mosaic, or a piece of music. The silences. Is that what you call them? The pauses. The erasures. Like chinks in the wall, in the armor. I'm sorry, I don't know anything about music terminology.

Do you remember those books about music, filled with music, sheets of music, which I couldn't read at all, from that bookstore in Tokyo, where you bought an armful? You understood some things that I couldn't. But there were also volumes of haiku. Maybe novels. Something for everyone. I don't know what the Japanese called what we bought. We bought those books because the paper was thick, deckled, gold-flecked. I would tear up the sheets and use them for something, eventually. That's what I said, but did I, ever?

In Kyoto, hotel employees sprayed water over their stone courtyards, washing away, several times a day, as a sign of welcome. Do you remember when we were foreigners?

We spent our money on travel and experiences. Dinners, bullfights, beaches. To shore up memories for later, to have something to look back on, when we're old and can't—

We had enough money back then, and we could have gone anywhere.

How much money do we have left? What if this goes on forever, with you in a bed? While I am still struggling to piece something together. To hold things together, rather. The doctors haven't told me anything.

I read in a magazine that the number one regret people have at the end of life is not having traveled.

Are you comfortable where you are? I wish I could see you. I wish I could bring you some music. Even though everyone knows that's impossible.

But what's happening here can't last much longer. My interrogation, I mean. I don't know about your situation.

Every day is a failure. No progress, no reprieve.

Who is going to win?

The tour groups have started to overtake our neighborhood. Chinese, Swedish, French. They seem happy to be here. They want to see the landmarks. They ask me where to find the golden bull.

There is an old man who sits on the steps of Federal

Hall and plays a Chinese instrument that I can't stand. I'm sorry.

We're sorry this has been dragging on for so long. We thought things would be resolved quickly. But, as you can tell, there are some problems. We need you to think about what you've told us already. Because we need something else. Can you recreate the situation to the best of your ability? Can you tell us everything? In your own words, nothing fancy.

I don't know what to add. What to retract. We were in the middle of things when we went to Paris. Also, Venice, yes. We were just tourists. We didn't do anything. But it was my fault that we went, on a moment's notice. Out of the blue. Into the blue. I can't remember what we were doing. But I'm the one who suggested Venice, yes, if that's what you're asking. I thought Venice would help my art. How could it not? I wanted to see the marbled papers and the glassblowing. My husband could compose anywhere. And he liked to travel. We didn't even tell my mother-in-law where we were going. We just wanted to get away. It was like a vacation.

Your mother-in-law has been asking about you, how you're doing.

What did you tell her?

That you're communicating, if not cooperating. We're taking it day by day.

The next instant, do I make it? or does it make itself? We make it together with our breath. And with the flair of the bullfighter in the ring. (Clarice Lispector)

I thought if I could learn how to blow glass, or something like that, that might be something. Do you know what I'm talking about?

We'll review the transcript later.

What do you want me to say here? Why do you have to keep asking me the same things repeatedly? Can we take a break?

How else to proceed? What would you have us do differently?

Everyone just wants to know what happened.

It isn't a mystery.

I want to know if my husband is alive or dead in the other box, the other room. Because I don't know what else to think. No one offers me condolences, in any case.

You know what you have to do if you want to get

out and see for yourself. You know what you did. Don't you?

One evening, a woman fell from our building. Out of the window of the twenty-second floor. She died, of course. I think she did it on purpose. She was at the end of her rope.

There was a white sheet over the body on the sidewalk when I got home. I had to use the service entrance because there were barricades out front. She lived alone, so there was nothing to say to anyone. What I mean is that there was no one waiting in the lobby under the giant chandelier. To be comforted.

I turned around, just for a moment, in Venice, on some steps, that's it. Something shifted, something moved. Someone fell down. I had always thought it would be me, to tell you the truth.

Have you wasted your education and taken advantage of your husband? Did you take things too far? Is that why you had to get out of New York?

What are you talking about?

Your mother-in-law says your art is degenerate.

I think she means derivative.

Are you happy with what you have or are you worried about what might happen next? And what are you trying to accomplish here? What do you hope to achieve?

I can't answer every question, not like this, not now. It feels like the middle of the night. It's too much, and why can't I go out for walk? And what about the dogs?

There was a blue plaque on a yellow wall. Little patch of yellow wall. A strip of wallpaper. That's it. That's all. Oscar Wilde is buried in Paris. We went to see his grave, with the sphinx. Also Proust. There was the smell of croissants from a bakery across the street. There was music, something I'd never heard before, from someone's open window. Who was playing what? Beckett was elsewhere, in another part of the city. We went all the way to visit his grave as well. His stone was gray. What was written on it?

Let's take a break. We'll wait until you get over this. No one can use it, whatever you're trying to say.

He knew that the very memory of the piano falsified still further the perspective in which he saw the elements of music, that the field open to the musician is not a miserable stave of seven notes, but an immeasurable keyboard (still almost entirely unknown) on which, here and there only, separated by the thick darkness of its unexplored tracts, some few among the millions of keys of tenderness, of passion, of courage, of serenity, which compose it, each one differing from all the rest as one universe differs from another, have been discovered by a few great artists who do us the service, when they awaken in us the emotion corresponding to the theme they have discovered, of showing us what richness, what variety lies hidden, unknown to us, in that vast, unfathomed and forbidding night of our soul which we take to be an impenetrable void. (Proust)

I need to get back to work. My collages are piling up. I am building up to something. And I need to move some things into a storage unit if it looks like we're going to move back to London.

I haven't told my mother-in-law about that, however. She would go crazy if we went to another country.

We were just tourists on vacation, running through Venice. For what reason? There was some wine, I don't know how much. We had eaten clams and risotto and figs. Or we had at some point. There was a puddle, a scarf. My necklace was too long. The night was like tarnish, but it wasn't too black, not at all, not so dark that we couldn't see what was happening. It wasn't too late.

When you were visiting your husband in the other room, why didn't you stay with him at night, all night? There was a reading light. You could have used that.

They said I couldn't stay. I had to go and come back, back and forth, day after day.

Well, that's not true. You could stay with him forever if you wanted to.

He wouldn't like that. He needs solitude in order to compose.

Is that what's he doing?

I don't know.

Do you think he'd rather be alone in his room?

I don't know.

Would you?

My room is overflowing with canvases. Because I'm still trying. To create a collage that works. Not something like music that dissipates. Something else, with a residue. A stickiness that you can't get rid of, no matter how hard you rub. Something hard, like a rock.

Like a stone, smooth, consoling.

Like a boulder, something to shoulder.

The collages are getting larger, more complicated, and I am using more color. But mostly they've increased in volume.

They tell me I shouldn't try to keep things to myself. Hoarding is a disease. They have decided to watch me for suicide attempts. They think I might have had enough. Things might be too much. They think I might do something else at this point. I tell them: Don't be ridiculous.

Tell us about Venice.

The polished marble steps. They were so steep. The slide down so easy. You wouldn't believe it. I was surprised to see someone slipping, so extensively, careening. There were oyster shells in the gutter, maybe. Does that matter?

I am careful not to say anything about how you might have flung yourself down the steps on purpose. Because then they would want to know why you did it. Why you tried. How could you have failed? And then, what about love, who and when, and I would have to make something up because I don't know what else to tell them.

But don't worry. I'm not going to say any of that. All I know is what I saw. Plus, I need the insurance money, if it comes down to that. I don't want them to think you wanted to get out of all this. What were you thinking?

They asked me if you were depressed, feeling trapped, struggling to get out, and I said, of course not. Why would anyone think that?

Sometimes you said you just wanted to live inside the music. You didn't care about our apartment or the neighborhood. You could live anywhere. New York or London, it didn't matter. Either side of the river. But we didn't fight about it. We could always move if we had to. We could always wait.

Can I have some magazines while I wait? I don't need scissors because I can tear with my hands. I'm an expert at it these days.

Not now, maybe later. We'll be back soon. You can listen to some music while we step away.

But I hate to wear headphones or whatever you call those things. How long do you think—

Wasn't there someone who sang about how it's got to end? (ELO)

A man on the street said the end is near. He didn't know me, however. He just said it, out loud, into the air.

Your mother-in-law says your husband made a lot of money. She says you've been living off of it for years. Buying expensive shoes and antique books. But you have no children and no career. She says you don't do anything. She says you are not a professional.

I don't know what else to tell you.

Your mother is telling them that I'm a bad influence on you. She says that the books I read should be banned. What she means is that I shouldn't waste my time, but how are they supposed to know what she's talking about? She tells them I am a fan of the bullfights. That I have stacks of old books that look like a health hazard. They are taking it seriously. They tell me that bullfighting is illegal in some areas. I tell them I try to read everything I can.

What about between the lines and the fine print?

We need to talk about the insurance money now.

All right.

You see why we have to ask. People don't just fall down the steps in Venice for no reason. Even if your husband was running. And why was he running? It doesn't make any sense. We always have to question the spouse. Also, there's a witness.

But no one knows anything! We were alone in the night. I don't think anything else is possible.

But someone saw something. One of you was wearing headphones? While the other one was trying to say something in the drizzle. It might have been something important, but things were muffled. Was there shouting? A scarf that could be used to strangle someone. It looked like a fight.

If I were a musician, no one would question my methods. Improvisation as proof of life.

There are some statements that can't help you now.

Who is this witness to my struggle?

We can't tell you anything about that.

How can you trust him? He might not have been there at all! He might be willing to say anything in order for something to happen. Do you know what I'm talking about? Is there a reward for coming forward?

Eyewitness accounts are extremely unreliable. I read it in a magazine. People, however, still believe them. An eyewitness account is still the main thing that makes or breaks a case, unfortunately.

Once, when we were mugged in New York, my husband told the police that the man had two guns, one in each hand. The man was Hispanic. The guns were black. I said the man was Black. The guns were silver.

The police made us write down our separate stories on canary yellow legal pads. They put us in separate rooms until we finished. We could stay for as long as we had to. We didn't have to come to a conclusion. Or an agreement. We just had to write it all down. What we could. We could stay all night. They didn't care. I remember that.

Those were the days.

I remember when we stayed in that chateau outside of Paris. The paint on the walls, pale yellow, was peeling, just a little bit. There was music all night. Not the kind you wrote. Something else, entirely. It kept us up until morning.

I'm sorry, I'm tired of all this, and I wasn't paying attention. Shouldn't I have been released by now? Can I have a cup of coffee?

Maybe later. For now, try to answer the questions that we actually ask. We don't have time to waste.

Why? Has something happened?

Not yet.

We went to Venice. To get away from New York, just for a little while, not forever, of course not. We'd been to Venice before. It was one of those places you could revisit. Tourists were never disappointed, supposedly. There were spectacles and vignettes. There were souvenirs. There were glass rings the size of hockey pucks with pink streaks. There were pastel necklaces and velvet scarves. There was espresso in tiny cups. That sounds good. I don't know how many times we've been, to tell you the truth. I don't know what else to tell you.

A travel magazine says there are some cities we love because they never change and there are some cities we love because they're always changing. Which one do you want to visit? Which one do you want to live in?

In Berlin, there was a museum where we tried to see Cleopatra's handwriting, just a short official phrase on papyrus. But it wasn't there. There was a photograph of the piece in its place on the wall. That artifact had been loaned out. The original was elsewhere. As always.

Your husband is in the perfect position to write a book. About a person who has been elsewhere but is now stuck in New York. Have you been trying to convince him to do that? Have you been trying to coerce him? Have you been abusive?

Of course not. I would never make my husband write a book.

I would never do anything if—

Wait a minute. What time is it? How long have I been here? How long do I have to stay? What do I have to say to secure my release? No one tells me anything.

There was an exhibit of Klimt paintings in town and I missed it. Now there is an exhibit of samurai swords. I would like to visit it. I would like to go now. Before that exhibit closes.

There was a man on the subway with a samurai sword and he cracked another man's head open.

I would like to learn how to fill the cracks with gold. The Japanese have a word for it.

There is no clock in this room. It feels like a casino. Fake plants, a few chairs, and some magazines that people have torn apart as if they were ravenous. Just like the waiting room in your hospital. Miscellaneous things, and things unraveling. Water stains on the ceiling. Has it been raining? Was it ever?

I feel like I'm talking to myself.

I mean, I feel like I need to do something else. My collages, that's something, and they need my attention. I think I can make something work. I have an idea for how to do it all again. I have an idea that might be perfect.

Your whole life, like a sandglass, will always be reversed and will ever run out again—a long minute of time will elapse until all those conditions out of which you were evolved return in the wheel of the cosmic process. And then you will find every pain and every pleasure, every friend and every enemy, every hope and every error, every blade of grass and every ray of sunshine once more, and the whole fabric of things which make up your life. (Nietzsche)

I don't care, I'm not giving in. I have all the time in the world. They can repeat the process if they don't believe me.

I feel like I'm talking to myself. I mean, I can't help it.

I would like to go home now and cook dinner. I wouldn't mind being locked up in our apartment forever. With an open window, some light, not too much, look out. But right now, I have to walk the dogs. I have to finish my work.

I have to finish what I started.

There is music coming in through the window. Someone is playing something on the saxophone. But I can't remember if you liked saxophone music or not. Why not?

The Japanese tourists can't get enough of it, that feeling of New York. They stop me on the sidewalk to tell me how much they love this city. Not as much as Paris, of course. Of course not. Don't be ridiculous.

Your time is almost up.
What?
This case is about to be closed.
How?

I always thought that if I were in your situation, confined, constrained, imprisoned, that I would panic. Struggle to get out.

Your mother-in-law is waiting for you in the hall. You've answered enough questions. Your responses will be compiled.

But what about the insurance company? Will they help me? What about the money? Some recompense for my trouble? Don't I have to sign something to prove my point?

I could live for a long time on that money, even in the middle of New York City. Do you think people will think it's suspicious? If I continue to buy yellow roses in winter? What about black pearls?

Where is my necklace? The pink glass that I came in here with? I am not prepared to leave without it. I am not prepared to live without something.

On the street, I can't decide. Should I go home now or visit your room? The weather has changed, and there are things to do. I will see you soon, as soon as possible.

Our apartment is near Thames Street, near Bridge Street, Stone Street, and Pearl. (Stone Street was the first street in New Amsterdam to be paved, 1658.) Bridge, Stone, Pearl. This city is so old.

This city is so hot, almost tropical. Do you remember when we first started, before you made any money, before I had any art, when there was a small hotel on Tortola? There were mangoes. There still are. A woman is selling them right now, cut up into slices, in plastic bags, on the street, in front of the subway. I would bring you something like that, something you used to like, if you could eat it.

I would cook you an entire dinner and make it last all evening.

Do you remember dinner on that terrace by the ocean? While watching the island with the ruins of the last leper colony on it? Grilled fish, white wine, and something. The waiter told us how the fishermen, moonlighting, long ago, went out to deliver things, raisins and games and butter, to the colony. Whatever the lepers wanted, whatever they could afford, whatever they could barter for. And then the waiter left us to ourselves, to eat dinner in silence. The summer air was a balm. Pink and warm. Slipping over our arms. The cooks splashed the leftover fish, skin and bones, into the water, or threw them onto the rocks. The waiters sang a little song.

Can you hear the things you've already composed? Can you remember music? At least you have music, or did, long ago. Your songs are still out there. I hear them, but I don't remember the titles. Do you recite to yourself all the names of the things you've accomplished, all the things you've loved? Do you keep a list? Does it help?

Do you hear what I'm saying? Are you taking it in? Is it sustaining you? Or are my words flowing around you, eroding you like a rock?

What's going to happen if you never finish what you started? If you never get to do what you always wanted? Because you know I can't do it for you. I don't understand music at all. I don't even know the proper terms. Notes and measures. Sharps and flats. But I know there's more than that. I'm sorry I don't understand. I don't even know how to open your files.

I concentrate on my own work. What else would you want me to do? What would you prefer?

Would you prefer another life? Another wife?

From where I'm sitting, it looks like you've done a lot. It's something to look back on and think about. Don't worry about getting the chronology right.

Do you remember what happened in Venice? Did you suspect me of something? Were you scared of a trap? You said we went to Italy because I suggested it, I seemed set on it, even. But you wanted to go, too, didn't you? You always liked to travel. You liked transportation. I hope you can remember that.

Your mother says it was all my fault. She wishes she had a different daughter-in-law. Someone professional, put together. Someone with accomplishments. I remember how you used to put on your headphones to avoid these conversations.

I wonder if they let you have any electronics in your room now. That would be wonderful. Are you still in a private room? Or do they make you share it with people?

At least you don't have to talk to them.

At least you're in New York. Where a bit of opera music might float in the through the window at any moment. There is the smell of garlic and beer. Chinese food, Caribbean food. Does it remind you of something? Your window faces a busy street. You could spend all day watching for something. Hoping for something. But what? What do you want? What do you think would do the trick?

You mother always said you should have been a conductor, rather than a composer. That would have been better.

Regret is a useless emotion. Have I told you already? I read it in a magazine.

Should I bring you a magazine? Would that be better

than a book? I could read from either one. I could read from anything, if that's what you want.

What about music? Should I try to sneak some in? What if it causes an explosion in your brain? Or in the room?

But they check me for electronics and weapons every time I visit. I can't do anything about that. So what do you want? What do you think?

Do you think you're going to be able to sleep through everything?

Either you will wake up and tell the truth or I will walk out, when the time comes, and collect the insurance money. No, that's not right. They've changed the policy. They said I didn't pass their test. Whatever it was. I didn't even know that I had taken it.

There were some blanks in the insurance form that weren't filled in correctly. They never explained the process. They didn't have to. They didn't say whether they blamed me or you.

I have some questions. But they say I can't expect any help.

Prepare yourself. No, don't worry, I'm talking about myself.

3

Blink if you can hear me. Blink twice. I'm sorry. I've been gone for so long. Should I try to say that it's not my fault? They wouldn't let me visit. They wouldn't even let me send a message through your mother. Who is fine, by the way. They also asked her some questions, but as you know, she doesn't know anything.

I should have been here sooner, but I couldn't manage it. I tried to carry too much on the subway. Something got caught in the gap. I won't even tell you what I lost. Concentrate on what I've brought.

You have no idea what it's like out there.

The things they were asking me about. The things I had to explain. The things I had to resort to. Insinuations, maybe. And then I had to extricate myself. How much do you remember? Has anything happened? I kept talking to you while I was away, as if you were in the apartment with me, or in the room where they interrogated me, or on the street, wherever, even though you couldn't hear me. Could you?

Are you going crazy?

How are you doing? Have you done anything lately? Have you done anything different? Have you been thinking about it at least? Have you done all you could? Has anyone said anything?

Every day, I went in and told them what I could. It was never enough. They said they were piecing it together. Building up to something. Like what?

You feel like an iceberg. Let me call the nurse.

But it's so hot in here, almost tropical. Your radiator is banging, and I can't stop it. I'm sorry.

Look, I've opened the window. Just a sliver. Can you hear the music? I don't know where it's coming from. Or what you'd call that instrument.

Is this my worst-case scenario or yours?

I always tried to prepare myself for whatever might happen. I always said I'd never be like your mother. Caught off-guard. Trapped. In a life that no one wanted. Even though this is the life she asked for.

Your mother is in the hall, talking to a doctor. Crying to the doctor. I try to comfort her, but I don't know what to say. Because this could go on forever.

She says I should keep the window shut in your room. The city air is so bad. Also, she thinks you need curtains. But what if you want to look out? What if you want a breeze, a breath of fresh air, a bit of sunset, the feeling of a squall coming over the ocean, almost capsizing the boat, that feeling of relief upon drinking one bright green cocktail when it's all over?

Your mother says that's not what you want.

Do you remember Verona? How people sat around in circles at bars outside in the autumn with their orange drinks that became fluorescent when backlit by the sunset? That was something, wasn't it? Maybe we could go back. Would you like that? Or Vienna. What do you think? Do you think you'll ever be able to exist in another place? What about a visit?

Sometimes a song from the past breaks through the window. Breaks something like glass. Someone on the street is playing it loud. It's that kind of music that can stop you in your tracks. I mean, me. Can you hear it? Do you feel it? Do you know what I'm talking about? Do you want me to close the window now and try to keep everything quiet? It doesn't matter what the weather is. I know you could never tolerate the kind of music that I liked.

Look: Someone brought you roses and balloons. I don't
know who. Can you see them? Should I move the bed?
The balloons say Get Well Soon. The roses are blue.

I'm sorry people are so unoriginal.

You're lucky. That's what everyone says. Most people
in your situation would be dead. This is not what usually happens to people who fall headlong down such a
steep flight of foreign steps. And it's a shame because
Venice is such a beautiful city. The seafood, the canals,
pink lights. That's what people remember. That's what
they tell me about. Always the pink. What do you think
that's about?

Blink twice if you want me to continue.

I'll come back tomorrow.

I'll tell your mother to come in from the hall.

Your mother has brought in some food. She knows you
can't eat it. She thought the smell would do you good.
She said to me: It's not for you.

I should have been here sooner, but I had to walk the
dogs. I walked them around the block, twice. They
didn't want to go inside. They wanted to play in the

snow. They can't get enough. And then I stopped at the deli for hot chocolate.

Your music was like snow, falling over the apartment, catching me off-guard, surrounding us with the sound of feathers. But I know that's not how you would describe it.

Do you want to talk about something else? You can tell me.

But I need to get out of this room, soon. I have other things to do.

When I'm not here with you, I'm in the apartment, doing my work, working on collages. I keep working, no matter what happens. The days are split. Between you and art.

Although I do other things, too. Someone has to clean out the closets and polish the silver teapot. Do you remember where we bought it? (Morocco)

Was it a mistake to have carried something like a teapot so far? Something so useless. But what else was there? What else could we do? I didn't know it would need so much polishing.

I'm sorry. Should I stop talking?

I know you always liked it when everything was quiet in the apartment. Then you could listen for the truth, or whatever you liked to call it.

One day I will find the right words, and they will be simple. (Kerouac)

Do you remember the dogs? On the highway in Vietnam. A truck passed by with cages piled up in the back, in the open air. Each cage was filled with dogs, stacked flat like pancakes, like chickens going to market. (Do you remember the signs for dog restaurants along the highway?) The truck sped up and the dogs moved on. Ears flapped in the wind. But the dogs weren't barking. They were not calling out to us to save them. Besides, what could we do? Except continue. Hope for a hairpin turn and a traffic accident. Which would allow some dogs, at least, the chance for escape, the chance to run out of their cages as the truck flips. But would any of them take advantage of it, this twist?

The doctor says we don't know if the fall caused your problem or if there was something that precipitated the fall. This could have happened anywhere. (Venice wasn't necessary.) It's not your fault. Do you know what I'm saying?

You feel so cold. I've brought in your long striped scarf. Do you remember it? Where we found it? What it cost? There was all that wine before dinner. And now: Are you starving?

Last night, I cooked something Italian. Pork belly with radicchio and hazelnuts. I've cooked it before, of course, and that cookbook is starting to look tattered, splattered with oil. I opened an old red wine. Plus, I had music in the background, and I sang along. Is it wrong to continue my life while you're still confined? And for how long?

I did not invite your mother, however. Because we can't help each other. She always wants to go over the same material. Venice and the steps that were so slippery. She has lapses. She can't remember. Were the steps really marble? Were they as white as milk or was there something else? She just can't understand it. What about bridges? And what were the chances? This shouldn't have happened. Things like this don't happen to people in a city as civilized as Venice.

Ezra Pound and Igor Stravinsky are buried in Venice, on the cemetery island, with its cypress trees, rustling, a respite. We took the boat out to see the graves. We traveled with the widows in long black dresses. Do you remember that trip? How many times have we been? Does it make you feel calm to think of an island? What about an island that's a cemetery?

But then later, not long after: you turned around and I reached out. I was saying something. But it was too late. That is, it didn't matter. That's what happened.

I was always talking—was it too much?—and you weren't listening. Or rather you were listening for something else. I don't know what, and you never explained it. You said I should go out and see for myself.

I didn't go far. I tried not to get lost. I stopped in stores like jewel boxes but never churches. I bought a green umbrella with a wooden handle that the clerk said would last a lifetime if I took care of it.

And then later, back together, those steps were so slick, opaline. Did you think that would be the last thing you saw or that you've ever seen?

What are you thinking? Are you composing? A response to everything I've said? That would be great.

Do you remember when we thought going to Italy was a good idea? I thought it would be good for my art. And you didn't mind traveling. We were both trying to do something. Something good, something grand, either way. Do you even remember what we said to people back then? We were struggling, but not really, not quite. What I mean is: hadn't we accomplished something already? Didn't we have enough? What more did we want? Do you remember that feeling?

We told other people we were just tourists, going on vacation.

Your mother said we should settle down. Some of the places we went made her feel embarrassed: Monaco, Waikiki, Tijuana. What would we ever achieve by traveling? She couldn't explain it to her friends, what we were thinking.

Do you remember the bullfights? The yellow sequins and the red capes. What did you think?

What was your favorite place? Should I try to guess?

We'd been to so many islands already.

In Capri, we walked to that villa on the hill and saw the small sphinx brought all the way from Egypt at some point, I think it was early twentieth century, but I can't remember everything, and situated on a terrace, overlooking the ocean. That sphinx had its face turned away from the tourists. It was impossible to see if the face was even still intact, after all that had happened. It was impossible to see, even if you leaned out over the ledge, over the water, and peered around its haunches. No one can lean out far enough, ever, over that water, that's what they told us later. Don't even try. You don't want to fall into the ocean.

I'll try again tomorrow. You know I always come back.

I put on my hood when I leave your room and hope not to run into people who want to talk about how you're doing. What you're doing. Are you doing anything? I can't tell. I can't tell them. Neighbors and doormen. They feel sorry for me. When I go out at night to walk two dogs.

On the street, sometimes, someone stops me. To ask for directions. Or to say how wonderful, this city. My dogs are so beautiful. A man from Japan said: Congratulations!

A man from Paris said I was extremely lucky to be able to live like that in a place like this at such a point in history.

Wasn't there someone who sang about how sometimes you've got to run? (Soft Cell)

How are you feeling? The nurse says you seem to

struggle sometimes when no one is looking, as if you're trapped and trying to get out. But that can't be right. What is she talking about? You can't move, we all know that. What are you trying to do? What do you want?

I'm sorry. You fell, and I failed to catch you.

I've brought you a souvenir from your room at home. Can you see it?

Can you feel it? It's the conch shell from the antique store in Copenhagen. I'll hold it close. It's the one with the carved scene on the outside and the silver inlay. I think you loved this thing. But there was a better one for making music. A thick pink one we pulled out of the beach. I still have it at home. I haven't given away anything. I haven't given anything up, not yet.

Kierkegaard is buried in Copenhagen in the same cemetery as his rival, celebrity author Hans Christian Andersen. Kierkegaard's stone is inscribed in a plain font. Andersen's is surrounded by purple pansies. Do you remember anything else about their graves? What did they say?

Do you remember the souk and the snakes under baskets and the croissants in the cafes surrounding the maze of stalls, where we bought the cheap silver teapot that we kept forever but never used? We never drank tea, only coffee.

And then the best croissants we ever had were in the subway station in Osaka. Better than in Paris. Do you remember that? I'm sorry, I'm going to stop asking you questions. I'm going to try to stop asking. Try to stop. I don't know if that's possible.

Earlier today, when I was walking over here, I stopped at that café on West Fourth Street and ate a croissant and had a cup of coffee. I'm sorry you weren't with me. I'm sorry I stopped without you, but I had to. I was starving. And then I went into a gallery, where a new collage artist had an exhibit. Cobalt papers streaked with bronze. Blurred words behind vellum. Scribblings under resin. Hybrid text paintings. That's what it said on the wall. The artist's statement. It looks like I'm going to have to try something else.

I've been producing more than ever. It's like I have more time and space and momentum than ever before. Do you think it's too much? So much linen paper in ivory and white. Rolls of mulberry paper from that Japanese store. Although I was working just fine before, when we were together. We were in the middle of things when everything happened. Things were proceeding, progressing, maybe. I don't know. How can you tell?

Maybe I shouldn't have said anything.

Do you think I should stop working while you're unable? Is it unfair? But it's all just text and paper. Do you wish I would stop talking about it? Do you wish I would stop talking entirely?

There is an exhibit of Chinese scholars' rocks in Midtown. The exhibit requests silence as you walk through. Would you like to see the catalog?

Walking over here, I watched the skyscraper glass turn from orange to green, like a tarnish, all of a sudden. You can see the shift happen, if you wait for it. There's just a moment, a flash. Like that green flash on St. Martin, when the sun sets into the ocean. Can you remember something like that? Did it make an impression? Do you know how it happens? How often?

A man walking in front of me, watching the same skyscraper, said to someone: "This looks just like that spaceship, with the two halves, perfectly symmetrical."

I read in a magazine that symmetry is one of those things that people crave. One of those things that makes faces beautiful. But it's rare for a face to be perfectly symmetrical. A mask, maybe.

Are your bandages too tight? You look like papier-mâché. Can I help you? You know you can tell me anything. You know I come here every day, right? I push open the heavy door of your room. Why are they always closing it? In any case, I come through. And now I am here for you. I am here. That's what I'm trying to say. That's all I'm saying for now.

Wasn't there someone who sang about how I'll be watching you? (The Police)

Should I sing you a song? Ha! No, I would never do that to you. I know you would laugh if you could. You could sing a song for me, of course, that would be good.

I read in a magazine that one surefire way to make yourself happier is to listen to music, even sad music, it doesn't matter. Do you think that's true? Does it work only with music? There must be something else you can use.

I can see the blank slate sky through your window. The top of a building is emerald. Can you see it from that position? Should I move your bed? It looks like Canary Wharf, doesn't it? A little bit. Maybe.

Do you still think about London? I mean when we used to live there. Not about whether we still could.

Do you ever think about where you'd like to go next? Where you'd like to end up? I know it's not with your father in Westchester. Do you ever think of composing your own epitaph? It's something to think about.

I won't mention that to your mother, don't worry.

I were miserable if I might not die. (John Donne's last words)

Do you ever think about a stone? A shell? Something to have and to hold.

Or something to make? Do you think you could make it yourself? I mean, could you make it on your own? If I had to go away.

I hope you're thinking about getting ready to leave this room at some point, preparing yourself, making a note of what there is to hold on to when you get out of bed. I'm talking about a handrail.

When I walk over here in the afternoons, I take a shortcut through the cemetery to avoid the tourists. It is always cool and dark on that path. A relief in this heat. There are no names I recognize on the stones. The stones are so old, inscrutable. I mean, illegible. So old and smooth.

The tourists are a hassle and you have to walk around them. But they don't go into a cemetery unless someone famous is buried there.

I read in a magazine that we should be thrilled to live in a part of town that tourists want to visit. Think of it as a privilege to walk out in the morning and be surrounded by so many and so much.

People line up for Neapolitan pizza that smells like Pompeii. Burning wood, coffee, charcoal. What more do you want? What more do you want to know?

Has your condition improved somewhat? Is there something else I should ask you about?

Blink twice if you want me to continue.

I'll come back tomorrow. You know that I come to see you every day, no matter what happens. This is what I do. Although I do other things, too, but I don't have to tell you that.

Do you want to see your mother or not? I'll tell her to come in from the hall.

Your mother never said who was staying with you while

I was away, in the other room. Your mother never told me anything. She says she doesn't know what to say. She doesn't understand. How can we all be here like this, stuck together, helpless?

Also, the tourists scare her. I mean, the terrorists. What if something happens? New York is a target. What if there's a blackout and you have to be evacuated? She asks me if I'm worried. I don't know what to tell her. She asks me how I'm doing. But it doesn't matter. She doesn't really care.

No one told me if you were alive or dead while they kept me in that black box of another room. I'm not sure how long. They weren't trying to torture me. They just wanted information. They didn't care about my position. If I was uncomfortable or inconsequential. They said I wasn't a prisoner. And they did let me go home at night, so that was something, and I should have been grateful. They said I was lucky. But they had to continue every morning, and I had to return. They had to write a report.

I told them what the doctor said: we don't know if the fall caused your problem or if there was something that precipitated the fall.

But they wanted to know it all.

What else do you want me to tell you? Maybe someone else's story would be better. Tell me what books you're interested in and I could read out loud to you in the afternoons. Someone suggested detective stories, but I can't remember: do you like mysteries?

Do you want me to open the window? There are cherry blossoms at the deli. There are birds, probably, again, out there. Pigeons, seagulls. How many kinds of birds exist in New York City?

What would you like to hear? You can tell me.

I know you don't want to talk about the weather, the seasons, some flowers, seagulls or whatever. Even though the Japanese are very concerned with seasonal references, and you loved some Japanese things, I know that, I mean, you always had something to say about Japan. Or am I wrong about that?

I'll try something else. We have to do something different, even if we fail. We have to talk about something. Do you know what I'm saying?

I am thinking of taking a flower arranging class (ikebana) while you are in bed. There is a school for it here in the city. New York has everything. We don't need to go anywhere else. The course description says: "Take in hand full your flowers."

During my interrogation, I didn't tell them anything about that, what our life was like. I wouldn't have done that. How could I?

And then their witness recanted (he might have been delusional), so their case is finished. No one thinks you did anything out of the ordinary. Maybe you were careless, but no one says I am to blame.

It's as if nothing ever happened. Our incident will be filed away, forgotten about, maybe even incinerated. Their conclusion: we were just another couple on vacation. And then there was an accident. It happens all the time. The kind of thing tourists get themselves into on a regular basis while traveling. I tried to tell them we were artists, not tourists. But in the end, they said they thought we hadn't done anything. That's what they wrote down.

The insurance people have decided, however, that I can't have any money. I filled out something incorrectly. Or you did. They didn't have the right information. There was something in the fine print that we never read, apparently. But there's nothing we can do about it now. Is there?

You'll be stuck here forever while I am unable to continue. That's one possibility.

I could try get a job, but we both know it would never pay enough. Or I could go somewhere else, but:

Travel as escape is a myth: I read it in a travel magazine.

Baudelaire said about Brussels: "There is nothing to see, and the streets are unusable."

What if we stay put?

In any case, I can't help you escape.

They always check me for electronics and weapons before I enter your room.

Or would you rather risk everything and keep moving? To die along the road is destiny: that's what Basho said. Do you know who Basho is? I hope so. He wrote some haiku.

Would you like to? Compose a haiku? Only a few syllables. You can do it. It's like music. Pretend you're in school.

My haiku manual says that you don't have to limit yourself to seventeen syllables if you're writing in English. You can do anything, really. Do you want to?

But I know: haiku is not like music, not really. I'm

sorry, I shouldn't have been talking about something like that, something that you don't like. I know what your blank looks mean by now. I am not going to force you to come up with a poem, of course not. Not on the spur of the moment. It would take some work, to make a seasonal reference and craft the cutting word. I wouldn't make you do that, not at this point in your life. Is it the end or not?

Do you want to tell me everything now? About what you wanted? What you wanted to have done with your work? What you were working on when everything happened. Do you remember? There was something in Venice, something you discovered about a songwriter who'd been discovered in a bland tower apartment in Paris, something about what she was thinking, what she was creating, something that changed her mind, something that made you stop. It was something she said. But you never had time to tell me what you thought it was about.

Is someone else going to want to hear your music before it's too late? Do you want to give me the password to your files? Is someone waiting for what you've done or not? Our money is about to run out, that's what I'm talking about.

But, obviously, this isn't about the money. Otherwise, I would have done something else by now, don't you think? Blink again so I know you really mean it.

Is there something else you want to tell me?

Sometimes I feel like I'm talking to you in a foreign language. No, I'm sorry, like I'm talking to you from another room. Or like I'm on the street, trying to be heard through a closed window.

If I look outside of your window right now, I can see columns and cobalt blue.

It looks like Athens, doesn't it? Do you remember the Temple to Poseidon where Byron scratched his name into a column?

Do you?

Just because you can't communicate (or, rather, won't) doesn't mean you can't think. I know that much. But I know you never liked to talk, even before all this. I remember how you used to wear those headphones around the city. I thought you were going to get yourself killed. I was scared that someone might take advantage of you while you were listening to something else, totally unrelated to what was happening around you.

But your life was always music. No one has forgotten that, what you were like, don't worry.

This is a disaster for you, isn't it?

You were a composer, and I was an artist, and we went to Venice. That's it. We went to Venice, as people have been doing for centuries. We were just going to escape, for a while, not forever, of course not: that's what we told people. We were tourists on vacation. I still use that line.

I continue to work while you're stuck in here, if you want to know the truth, if you want to know what I'm doing.

And in all things that live there are certain irregularities and deficiencies which are not only signs of life, but sources of beauty. (Ruskin)

We were in the middle of things when everything happened. We left New York and went to Paris. Also, Venice, yes.

And what about Rome? I almost forgot about that. The Caravaggios at the back of the church. We went to admire the chiaroscuro effects. And then we left and went to a bar to drink tiny cups of coffee while standing up. I looked out at a fountain, while you listened for something. I don't know what.

I listened to someone else's conversation. Half in German. Someone was talking about how to compose a life rather than a painting. A painting was not enough. One needed to do other things, too. Travel, for example. That's the advice that someone gave someone.

Maybe we should have never left New York. Your mother always said we were crazy. Living like gypsies. With our dogs in the bedroom. No proper office to go to every morning. Traveling for no reason. What was the point of life if it didn't produce something? She didn't say it quite like that. And why would we ever go to Japan, halfway around the world? Your mother had no desire to see somewhere like that. She had lived through the war.

Can you imagine life without Japan? Also, the other places. I don't know which one was the most important, what we couldn't live without. There were so many places, weren't there? We had to try. Who knows where we would have the best chance. The best choice. But then we always came back to New York. I don't want to put words in your mouth, but we always agreed on that.

Or did you prefer the castle near Nara? Where the

ninjas used to hide in the wall panels for hours, waiting for something to happen. Waiting for someone.

There are safe rooms that can be installed inside an apartment. I read about it. If you're scared of things. You can fill it with food and monitors. A walk-in closet can be retrofitted. But we never had a walk-in closet in New York City, did we?

I always thought that if I were in your situation, then I would panic. Struggle. But I don't know. I have done my best. What else is there to say? Are you alive or dead in there?

I remember Pompeii. Raisins like gravel in the museum. Blackened figs. We had been eating figs in Venice, before all this happened. That much, at least, is believable, isn't it? I mean, that's what I tell people.

Does it help to remember things? Things that are so far away, so foreign. Even our apartment. You haven't been there in so long. I've taken over your music room. I've put the audio equipment into storage. I can get it back for you at any time, of course. I've kept your conchs lined up on a shelf. I didn't know what else to do with them. I remember conch fritters on the beach in the dark. A vat of oil for frying.

There are other things as well. There are other things scattered around the apartment. Or stacked up on shelves, between the books. I can bring things to you, for you, if you want. I can put them by your bed.

Will it make a difference? I don't know what to do for you, here at the end. I'm sorry. Should I make a fresh start, restart, refresh?

Begin again? That's what I'm saying. That's what I'm asking, but you don't have to answer.

Those polished marble Venetian steps. Polished by so many feet. So slippery. They were so steep. The slide down so easy. I was surprised to see someone slipping, almost elegantly, momentarily.

I wonder if you did it on purpose.

And now, is this where you thought things would get you? How long are you prepared to go on like this? What am I going to do without you? What do you want me to do? And what will happen to your mother? You know I can't help her.

Would it have been better if you'd died in a robbery? A slash to the neck and then you wouldn't have had to say anything. There were parts of Venice that were shady, shadowy. That still are, maybe. And we were sometimes flashy, not too much. We could have gotten into trouble.

On my way over here, down a side street, a man came toward me, walking fast, playing loud music from a long time ago. He caught me off-guard. I panicked. Tried to get away. But he was playing that music at top volume. There was no way.

Wasn't there someone who sang about how I think I would die? (Bee Gees)

We still have some time left. All afternoon, even. That's what I think.

You always said you'd rather die than see a Broadway musical.

I'm sorry, I know you hated the music I listened to. You preferred something undiscovered. Something like a question that couldn't really be answered. That's what kept you going. Maybe there was a Japanese word for it. Maybe something in German.

At the end of life, a Japanese person might write a death poem in order to say something, one more thing, knowing it's the last thing. Not necessarily a haiku. There are all sorts of impulses and reasons. There are many kinds of farewell. Not every poem is successful.

Do you think it's a good time to write something now? I know words are not music, but maybe they're better than nothing? You can blink, and I can translate. I'll write it down. It might be good for you. I don't know. I don't know what I would do if I were you.

And I've been wrong before, of course.

Also, when you fell, I failed to catch you.

What would I do if I could? What would I do if I can't?

There is an article in a magazine about how to write your own obituary, as an exercise. Not for someone else to use, when the time comes, just something for yourself, to see where you're headed. There's also an article about how to write your own epitaph.

Your mother says I shouldn't talk to you about things like that. She says I am a fatality. She means fatalistic. But that's not what I am.

Maybe I should be quiet for a while. Don't say anything.

I've been thinking about Alhambra, in the moonlight,

how quiet it was. Maybe that's something you would like to think about now. Do you remember how we felt special? Only a few other tourists were with us because the nighttime visit required extra tickets. White stone flowers. The serenity of calligraphy. Was there something about infinity? I can't remember. Columns like palm trees surrounding the stone lions in their courtyard. The smell of oranges in the dark. The smell of lemons. You heard sounds in the distance, something sporadic. Violence? Because Federico García Lorca, for one, was shot not far away. But that was another time, and these sounds were something else.

I know you liked the silences in a piece of music. The spaces in between. Fill in the blanks—no, leave them empty, that's what you liked. I always preferred the other parts, the symbols and shapes. Notes, notations.

Your mother says I shouldn't make you think about the past, or the future, because how do I know what will happen?

Long ago, when we first started, there was a small hotel on an island. I think it was Tortola. White seabirds making circles, making noise. You said it was impossible to track all the sounds. You could spend a lifetime looking for one strand to pick out. We could spend a lifetime in a circle of sand. It looked like a bullring. Or a traffic island in Manhattan. Broadway.

You were hoping to find a conch to keep. Were you writing a song?

I wish I could bring you some music. But they keep talking about interference. They say they never promised anything. To me or you. I don't know what to do.

T

What? Are you trying to say something? Are you trying to say my name?

I am here with you, don't worry. I leave at night, but I always come back. Your mother is here in the mornings. Don't worry about that.

Your mother wishes I was the one who fell instead of you. She keeps insisting on this to various people. Because I was the one who suggested we take off to Paris, at a moment's notice. Then Budapest, even Venice.

She doesn't understand how I can keep going. Because I am like a widow, almost. How can I keep working?

She says collages are for people who can't appreciate real art. Collages don't count if no one buys them. She wants to know what my collages are all about. I tell her she can see for herself.

Your mother asks me if I'd rather be a painter. And I tell her no, of course not.

Your mother asks me, sometimes, how I can keep going when you are stuck in a bed. It isn't fair. What you are doing? That's what she says.

I tell her the usual things. I don't elaborate. And I am not a comfort to her.

But I was never a comfort to her before all this happened. So it's the same.

She sometimes tells me about other artists who are famous. But look at you, she says.

I don't know what she says to you, when she sits by your bed, when I'm not here to help you. Is it a torment?

I don't know what she does in the evenings. When you are left on your own, momentarily, free.

In the evenings, I go home and do some work. Cut and paste. Words on paper, but not my own words, necessarily. It doesn't matter. Streaks of yellow. Then I make dinner, maybe shrimp poached in olive oil with asparagus. Walk the dogs, read a book, look at my gold leaf in the dark.

New York looked very beautiful on the lower part around Broad and Wall streets where there is never any light gets down except streaks. (Hemingway)

I've been producing so much lately that it's become a fire hazard. Too much clutter and canvas. People die under the weight of their things sometimes. I read it in a magazine. Sometimes, someone can't get out. Hoarding is a disease. Having too much stuff is the same as having too little. Both paths lead to confusion. So what is the solution?

And how about you? Anything?

What about music? Can you ever have enough? And the places: Lisbon, Oslo, Saigon. Where we went looking. All the islands and the cities, nothing in between. We agreed about a lot of things. We knew what we had to do back then.

TEMP

Are you saying it's too cold in here? You feel like the tip of an iceberg.

Wait a minute, maybe I didn't understand. Can you say it again?

Take your time. I called the nurse. Someone will be here soon to take your pulse.

I remember St. Lucia, where the sand was so hot you couldn't even step on it. You tried to record the sizzling of the conch on the grill. The frying of fritters in a vat of oil. The sailor blowing into a conch on his boat. You were going to record all of it. Then distill it. Do you remember that, and is that what you called it? All those conchs we took. And the little boy who said to pay whatever price we liked. And we did, then we ran, through the rain, which had appeared out of nowhere. Steaming up streets. Mist spreading over the beach. I don't know where we thought we were going.

Can you hear the rain now, whipping your window? They say a hurricane is coming. So we might have to hurry. Prepare for a blackout, and all that. But that's all right. I have put some candles in your nightstand.

We can pretend we're elsewhere, living in another century, about to eat dinner. Snails and garlic. Bowls of pasta. Wine to knock us out.

TEMPO

Wait a minute. What?

TEMPO

Are you talking about music now?

I'm writing this down as fast as I can. Translating.

Doing what makes sense from where I stand/sit. You know I don't know anything about music. The terms, the forms.

I'm sorry. I get so impatient, even though I know you're doing your best.

What I mean is that the delay is driving me crazy. Every time you say something, I have to stop and figure it out. Consult the chart. But that's all right. I'm glad you're talking, if that's what you want to call it. That's what I'm here for.

I'll be back tomorrow.

The hurricane never came, so someone can erase that giant X from your window. It makes you look like a target. I will say something to someone later. But the rain is still falling. Can you hear it? There might be a leak from the ceiling. That drip would drive me crazy. I'll try to move you to another position.

When it's time to go, I'll put up my hood and run, don't worry.

Do you want to pick up where we left off?

TEMPO

Are you trying to say you want me to go slower?

Would you like to stop everything and compose

something, even if only for a moment? Even if only for yourself?

Wait a minute. Would you like to compose yourself?

I've brought in a tiny statue of Ganesha for you. The one we bought in New Delhi. Do you remember? I've put it by your bed. You can pray to it if you want. Ganesha is the god of obstacles and success, among other things. Although I know you're not going to pray to it. I wouldn't. But is there anything better than aluminum? Anything else in the apartment that I can carry? Something else I can bring you? I know you love certain things, I'm sure of it. Other things, too, maybe.

Of course, I still love you. But I can't tell you what to do. No one can tell you anything.
    Wait a minute, that's not true.

I remember when we stayed in that white chateau outside of Paris. There was music all night. Not the kind you wrote. It seemed to go on forever. We felt a little desperate.

T E M P O

Slower than this? Do you want things to stop? Do you want me to go home?

You always said music was a process of elimination. Are you trying to tell me something?

I can see the orange sky through your window. The teal river. People are walking by, wet and black. Umbrellas are up. The wind has died down. No one stops to look in here, however. Why would they? I will have to go out there and join them, soon enough, maybe.

Should I stay? Wasn't there someone who sang about something like that? (The Clash)

I have brought you the raven fetish with the turquoise eyes that we bought in Arizona. On that dusty road that smelled like red pepper. The sound of drums in the distance. The raven is a trickster, reminding us to transform. Maybe I should have brought you the bear?

TEMPO

Again? You know you keep saying the same thing forever? I feel like I'm talking to myself. And I'll have to go home soon. I have work to do.

I'm doing my best. Working with text and paper.

TEMPO

I've already written it down, what you said. See? What else?

I'm glad you're talking because everyone has been waiting for something to happen.

Do you have a solution, a resolution, a conclusion? I don't know what you call it in music.

Can you say something else? I know it's a struggle. Can you add something to what has already been said? I don't know what you want to tell me. I don't know what you want me to tell people.

And when you can't come up with the next line it doesn't mean you're old, it means you're dead. (Charles Bukowski)

Okay, I understand. Close your eyes for a while. I will drink my coffee. Pull pages from magazines. How many magazines are still in existence? I think there is less paper on the streets these days, less flutter, less litter. Fewer plastic bags caught in the trees. The streets are so empty this afternoon. Nothing to see out there, not now. Maybe later.

Okay now: some buildings are turning pink in the

sunset. But can you see it? It looks like someone has put up a curtain over your window. Some sort of gauze, maybe linen. Did the nurse do that when I wasn't here? You can see through it somewhat but not enough. Don't worry. I'll take it down later. Do you think your mother will notice the difference?

My collages look like that linen covering the mummies in the British Museum. My work has started falling apart. The glue was defective. Maybe I shouldn't have been stockpiling canvases, putting them on top of each other. Maybe I should have found a climate-controlled storage unit. Maybe I shouldn't have been trying to have everything. Maybe I should have gone in a different direction.

Outside, I catch a sign for flights to Iceland out of the corner of my eye.

There are other things I could tell you. What would you like to hear now? Your face is like a mask. Are you happy?

What are you trying to accomplish? Would you like something to hold onto? I could bring you another souvenir. Would that help? Or would it add to the confusion? The clutter in this room.

I know it's difficult, but I'm not going anywhere. Tell me again. What do you think? What do you want? We can repeat the process if necessary.

Do you want to touch a conch? Do you remember what one sounds like?

Will it be music to your ears if I hold it up for you?

Your mother is talking to someone about moving things around. Fixing things up. Sweeping out. She would like a better view for you. She is trying to do something. I don't know if it's working. I don't know what it's costing her. She says: My son, how he is doing? I don't know what other people tell her.

Do you feel better? They've changed your medicine. And your bandages. Your skin is less papery, maybe. What about a balm? Do they offer you something?

The doctors are saying that you might have to stay here forever.

There is a new redness, seeping, around the edges of your window. There is a bright sign outside, but I don't know what it says. I can't read it right now.

Maybe something happened. Can you hear that beeping? I think it's coming from your bed. Do you want me to move you to another position?

What's going to happen if you never finish what you started? If you never get to do what you always wanted? Because you know I can't do it for you. I don't understand music at all. I don't even know the words for it.

I know you're not asleep. It's too early for that. Are you trying to tell me to go home? Do you want to be alone? Who doesn't? Are you saying you've had enough? That you've done enough, that is. Leave everything as it is?

What do you want to do?

Do you want me to continue?

Does this room seem to be closing in on you? Plus, things are a mess. The magazines have been shredded. I will have to go soon.

I'll see what I can do.

TEMPOR

Just because something is temporary doesn't mean it isn't serious.

Just because something is temporary doesn't mean it isn't beautiful.

Wait a minute, I'm sorry. Maybe I shouldn't improvise.

Maybe I shouldn't fantasize.

TEMPO

I think I know what you mean. The more times you say something, the more it seems to make sense. Is this why you use repetition in your music?

I know you never understood how I lived, what I did. What could I do?

Could you survive without me? If I accidentally fell down the longest flight of subway stairs in the city, for example? On my way over here one afternoon. What would you do then? A sign on the subway says: Don't become a statistic.

How long can you stay here? I know you always wanted to live in Paris. Or was it London? Do you remember what you called it? Do you remember what you told me?

In London, the sign on the Underground said:
Danger: keep everything
clear
of the doors.

The doctors say there is always a danger. You're not out of the woods yet.

Where is the exit? And who can remember all the evacuation procedures? Or what to do if there's an active shooter running through the hospital? There was a handbook that we were supposed to read. In order to be prepared. In order to pass their test. There's a drill that they put people through. Even visitors.

If life is an exam to be taken, then maybe we haven't read the right texts.

I've torn up all the old books to use in my collages. I'm sorry.

TEMPO

Wait. I know what you're thinking.

If you're making music right now, you know that I can't hear it, right?

What I mean is: I should have brought you a chart of notes that you could reference, that you could make sense of. You could have sent a message. Would that have worked? Instead of an alphabet? Was there a better way and now it's too late? No, there's still time, maybe. What do you think?

Although you might have made a mess of things either way.

TEMP GO

Are you trying to say that I should hurry up?

Are you making a joke?

Do you want to hear about my work? I've done a lot. There's still a lot to be done, of course.

TEMPT O GO

Okay. I'll take what you say. Whatever you say, it's not a problem. I'll make it work. I'll figure it out. Translate/transpose. Whatever it takes. Don't worry. You can keep going.

Can you see the city from where you are? The buildings look like origami now. There are no sirens for a moment. There is a faint purple streak along the horizon that is holding everything together.

In the dark purple sea around Capri, the Sirens enticed sailors to shipwreck. That was the place, more or less.

You always said you were happy to visit any island or any city. You would go anywhere with me. So we did. We did everything. Didn't we?

You should at least try to stay awake while I'm here with you. I know you'd like to listen to some music, I know you have your heart set on it, but that's something I can't give you.

Do you want to talk about something else? I'm working on my collages when I'm not here with you.

But not everything has to be about art. Is that true?

I could have lived a long time on that insurance money, even in the middle of New York City.

What you are doing? That's what your mother asks me, not often. She means when I'm not here with you. What are my plans for the future, and how can I live without you?

She doesn't understand why we had to go on vacation, to Venice, of all places. We'd been before. How many times? What were we thinking? All of her friends' children have lives with awards and accomplishments. All of her friends' children have children. She thought it was my fault. She says I ruined your life. Her life, that's what she's talking about.

It was autumn, wasn't it, when we went? We'd been before, of course. But you said there were plenty of things you loved to do more than once. We could go to

Venice every year. If that's what I wanted. You would have done anything for me. You always did.

There was a palazzo apartment we rented for an entire month. Slightly decayed but that's okay. Things shimmered in the evening. Figs in hammered bowls. Gold-rimmed glasses. Chandeliers, etc. Maybe we drank too much. I can't remember. There was so much space. We had to fill it up. You worked in one long dark room. While I worked, too, I did my best, on another floor entirely, with paper spread out to the horizon. We each had something. But art wasn't a competition. Was it?

Is that saxophone on the corner driving you crazy? I passed by it on my way over here, after the mariachi band on the A train. They stayed in my car for the whole ride. They didn't move on, even though they weren't making any money. But I didn't move either. They were loud, and the music was bad. When I finally got out of the car, I heard someone say to someone else: It doesn't matter how long it takes. We're here now.

I'm sorry, I'm trying. Say it again, and I'll pay more attention. I try to follow your gaze. Are you looking out of the window? Are you hoping to see the river or the ocean?

I keep thinking about that castle in Nara, about how

that would have been better. People fall down steps in Japan all the time. All that slick wood with white socks. Everyone would have understood. Everyone still can.

The samurai prepared for their work by imagining death in every instant, so as to live to the hilt, with no regrets, in every moment. That's what I read in a book.

That would have been something, if you had fallen in Japan. It would have been our last trip.

I have a magazine that says people remember the end of a vacation more easily than the beginning. Forget about how it started. The ending is the main thing. But now I've put that magazine away. No more reading. It's just me and you. You can say anything.

TIME TO GO
What? No.
I don't want to leave you here, like this, like that, you know what I'm talking about.

TIME TO GO
Where?

TIME TO GO

Who? Me or you?

You know I still love you. Not right now, necessarily, but previously, yes. I would have never left you. We were always together, more or less. And there was always something to keep us going. One thing or another that we held on to. Something that we couldn't avoid.

Wait. There's one more thing. Something else. Isn't there?

The dogs are with the doorman, playing in the courtyard. Your mother is going to pick them up later. For a visit. She is going to try. She is going to trial, she said. She is desperate for visitors.

Wait a minute. I have an idea for another collage. It's perfect. I mean, perfectible. The background is white and slick, like lacquer, slippery. And then something is inscribed. As if into stone. If it's writing, you might need a magnifying glass to make it out. It might take a lifetime. A scribble from afar, but up close, something else entirely. Do you know what I'm talking about? It's hard to describe, but I could keep trying. The format isn't large. It could fit in one palm. Like a pebble. Portable. Like a paperback.

Some things you thought would come together in one space, like a song. Only a few minutes to sing, from beginning to end. Although you can keep singing it, of course, on repeat. That might be annoying to people but who would stop you? Or what about a bit of music without any lyrics? That's more like it. Like something you'd write, like something you'd like.

What do you think?

Wait. You have something in your eye. Don't blink. Okay.

THESE ARE THE TIMES THAT TRY. AND HOW. AND NOW. THE COAST IS CLEAR. DO YOU WANT TO GO DIVING? ARE WE EVEN ON THE RIGHT SIDE OF THIS ISLAND? THESE ARE THE TIMES. FLIES IN THE SUMMER. HOW LONG CAN YOU STAY UNDER? BEFORE COMING UP. BEFORE COMING UP WITH SOMETHING. LIKE PEARLS OR SPONGES. THEN? THE QUICK BROWN FOX JUMPS. NO ONE EVER SAID WHEN. NO ONE EVER SAID WHAT. THE LAZY DOG. NO ONE EVER DID ENOUGH. OVER. WHAT I WANT TO KNOW IS.

How did we make it back here? From Venice. What airport? I've almost forgotten what it feels like to fly. You had a scarf wrapped around your neck, so long that it was trailing through the puddles. I thought it might strangle you. And there was one pink necklace, glass or something else, that I held on to. I didn't want to lose it. I wouldn't let them take it. I wanted to keep everything. Who knows what we would need? To make something of ourselves. You always said we should invest. Save something. How else? And how we used to travel. How we lived. How did we? Those were the days. Do you remember how to say goodbye in Italian? Your mother must have arranged our return. She is fluent in several languages. Because preparations were made. Emergency evacuation and extraordinary measures.

But it doesn't matter how we got here. Only what we do. Are you ready? Things don't have to be simultaneous.

It doesn't matter how we got here. Only what we do next. What steps.

What have you done? your mother wails.

WORKS CITED

1

Anais Nin, *The Diary of Anais Nin, Vol. 3: 1939-1944*, ed. Gunther Stuhlmann (New York: Harcourt Brace Jovanovich, 1969).

Jacques Derrida, *The Gift of Death,* trans. David Wills (Chicago: University of Chicago Press), 1996.

Paul Bowles, *The Sheltering Sky* (New York: Vintage, 1990).

Leo Tolstoy, *The Kreutzer Sonata and Other Stories,* trans. David McDuff (New York: Penguin, 2008).

Yamamoto Tsunetomo, *Hagakure: The Book of the Samurai,* trans. William Scott Wilson (New York: Kodansha, 1979).

2

Gabriel García Márquez, quoted in *The Far Edges of the Fourth Genre: An Anthology of Explorations in Creative*

Nonfiction, ed. Sean Prentiss and Joe Wilkins (East Lansing: Michigan State University Press, 2014).

Walter Benjamin, "The Work of Art in the Age of Mechanical Reproduction" (1935), trans. Harry Zohn, in *Illuminations,* ed. Hannah Arendt (New York: Schocken, 1969).

Franz Kafka, *Letters to Ottla and the Family,* ed. N. N. Glatzer, trans. Richard Winston and Clara Winston (New York: Schocken, 1987).

Michel de Montaigne, *The Complete Essays,* ed. and trans. M. A. Screech (New York: Penguin, 1993).

Clarice Lispector, *Aqua Viva,* trans. Stefan Tobler (New York: New Directions, 2012).

Marcel Proust, *Remembrance of Things Past,* Vol. 1: *Swann's Way* and *Within a Budding Grove,* trans. C. K. Scott Moncrieff and Terence Kilmartin (New York: Vintage, 1982).

Friedrich Nietzsche, "Notes on the Eternal Recurrence" cited at https://ironick.medium.com/the-perpetual-novelty-of-sisyphus-7f8a7bf35bbf

3

John Donne's last words, as recounted by Edmund Gosse in an introduction to Donne's "Death's Duel"; cited at www.exclassics.com/duel/duel003.htm

Jack Kerouac, *The Dharma Bums* (New York: Penguin, 1986).

Charles Baudelaire, cited in *The Writer of Modern Life, Essays on Charles Baudelaire* by Walter Benjamin, ed. Michael W. Jennings, trans. Howard Elland et al. (Cambridge, Mass.: Belknap, 2006).

John Ruskin, *Selected Writings,* ed. Dinah Birch (New York: Oxford University Press, 2009).

Ernest Hemingway, *The Letters of Ernest Hemingway, Vol. 2, 1923-1925,* ed. Sandra Spanier et al. (New York: Cambridge University Press, 2013).

Charles Bukowski, *On Writing* (New York: Ecco, 2015).

ACKNOWLEDGMENTS

Thanks to the following publications, where a few paragraphs of this book originally appeared as parts of other works:

"Aficionado" in *Glassworks*
"Aftermath at the Museum with Fragments of Sappho" in *Ink & Coda*
"Mirror Finish" in *American Literary Review*

Many thanks to my family and friends for support of all sorts, especially to my husband, Dan, and to my parents (Billy and Sharon) and siblings (Danny, Holly, and Allison) for always pretending to like whatever I write. And a very special thanks to my mother-in-law, Melania, who is not the mother-in-law in this book but whose different views, values, and language helped create this bit of fiction.

Even more thanks to my editor at Regal House, Pam Van Dyk, for her careful attention to this text, and to my publicist, Laura Marie, for all of her work to get this book into the world.